ROCKETSHIP NATION

ANTHONY JASWINSKI

iUniverse, Inc.
NEW YORK BLOOMINGTON

Rocketship Nation

iUniverse books may be ordered through booksellers or by contacting:

iUniverse
1663 Liberty Drive
Bloomington, IN 47403
www.iuniverse.com
1-800-Authors (1-800-288-4677)

Because of the dynamic nature of the Internet, any Web addresses or links contained in this book may have changed since publication and may no longer be valid. The views expressed in this work are solely those of the author and do not necessarily reflect the views of the publisher, and the publisher hereby disclaims any responsibility for them.

ISBN: 978-1-4401-6884-0 (sc)
ISBN: 978-1-4401-6882-6 (dj)
ISBN: 978-1-4401-6883-3 (ebk)

Printed in the United States of America

iUniverse rev. date: 9/11/2009

For Amy

The engine was idle, difficult to hear through the wind. He climbed out the Firebird, shirt off, jeans still wet from the flash downpour that had come and gone on Dixie Highway. The air smelled of coconut salt and he could hear the traffic of A1A and the surf beyond.

He was shaking, fueled by the Nighttrain. The gash in his forehead was long clean of blood and sand and it stung. The pain in his back had grown weak from liquor. A sensation numb and sickly had covered his body, encapsulating him. He couldn't walk, only stumble across the pavement.

The Colt .33 was caught in his jeans buckle. He fought around his waist, pulling the gun out, nearly dropping it in the puddles of dirty rain. It was glistening, wet, appearing like a toy in the light of the streetlamps.

The store's neon sign spelled SAVE it ALL, glowing lime-green, looming over the lot.

The Nova's engine was running. He could make the form out through the car's heavy tint, hunched over, staring down at the steering wheel. He was an apparition. Made real only by the tiny glow of the Nova's interior light. His head, hung low, gave the impression of a man asleep.

He wanted him awake, to see the gun's barrel on the window; to hear the discharge as the bullet tore through glass and penetrated his face. The image energized him and he quickened his pace.

Forms, vicious and quick, darted around inside the convenience store. He could hear swearing, things breaking. He raised the gun. It was heavy to handle.

Wind blew across the pavement, scattering trash across the Nova's grill. There was a moment when it appeared beautiful and perfect, like autumn leaves in a backyard. It threw a chill over him so strong that he felt as if he had been thrown into deep water. He put his finger to the gun's oily trigger.

He thought about the crow.

He raised the gun to the driver's window and fired two shots.

JANUARY 28TH 1986
11:42 A.M.

They sat on the edge of the Westerfield condo dock, far apart from the rows of shoebox apartments and deepwater boat slips. A crane, rusted yellow, skeletal, sat in a patch of black dirt where it had been abandoned for the last three months. There were newer condos, half-finished, fractured in the morning sunlight. They appeared utilitarian. Formless against the chalk-white beach.

Rusty Vay took a drag of the joint and coughed. The pot tasted bitter and manufactured, laced with chemicals, insecticides he'd have found under a kitchen faucet.

Harlan watched the morning waves. They formed crisp lines, cutting northward in the early-morning break. The formation was good for January, long and defined. The morning cold left frost on car windows parked in the lot and there was the distant hum of space heaters from the open screen door of the condo's communal pool clubhouse.

From their vantage point, they could see the north end of the beach where dunes, sprinkled with pine grass, ended at a deep-water jetty. Kids raced across the pedestrian bridge, scouring for bits and pieces of the wreckage and some had paddled out with their boards, anxious to beat the search choppers.

A stomach virus had been acting up, sending tremendous heartburn into Harlan's chest and the marijuana had added only slight relief. He had grown tired gazing at the cloud of chemicals that sprayed across the winter sky. The shuttle's discharge, fresh from explosion, had given the sky colors that had begun to wear thin. The canvas of off-whites and cotton-candy pinks he'd witnessed only moments beforehand had gradually dulled; diminished now, an afterthought.

Rusty wiped his nose, bright red, wet from a cold he'd caught surfing the waters off Fort Pierce. His voice carried a frail, nasally hiss like a broken bicycle horn.

"What'd you say before?" Rusty asked. "About dolphins?"

"That they're smart." Harlan ran his pen over the spiral notebook's front cover.

"You said something else, about the research facility in the Keys."

"I never talked about the Keys, Rusty." Harlan felt his face. His skin was cold, but sunburned from the strong rays off the ocean water. December and January had been clear of clouds and the sun was stronger than he had imagined. "I was talking about Sea World. They do all this amazing shit there."

Yeah," Rusty said. "Like flipping around."

"No, I'm talking about their research facility branch. That's where they teach them to talk." He looked into the ocean, searching for the bottlenose pack Rusty had spotted earlier. He had not seen a dolphin all winter. He told Rusty that a dolphin was man's best friend.

"I thought the dog had that honor."

"That's what I thought," Harlan said. "She told me dolphins are better friends 'cause they'll save you from sharks."

"Who said that, Dana Dillon?"

"No." Harlan endured a stomach pang and he wished the marijuana to settle into his stomach.

"Dana Dillon gave head to Mr. Arlinger," Rusty said. "You believe that shit?"

Harlan coughed. The heartburn was stronger and his eyes stung from the pot and he had to blink. "It wasn't Dana Dillon. Lemme finish my story."

Rusty took a drag of the pot.

"She said they're gentle and unthreatening to their own kind. Almost always travel in the same packs since they were young. I liked the idea of them being all unthreatening."

"Why you think that is?" Rusty asked.

Harlan went quiet. He began to sketch portions of the beach. "I don't know. She thinks it's because they don't have hands."

Rusty stared at the slab of white smoke cutting across the sky. It altered, warped into shapes he imagined as firetrucks and playground slides; picnic tables and laundry.

The wind had begun to stretch and toss the chemical cloud west.

Rusty wondered how fast it was moving. The marijuana was blurring his vision and he decided the cloud wasn't moving at all and he shook his head. He told Harlan he was stoned and that he didn't know what he was talking about.

"I thought about it," Harlan said. "In Iran, if you steal, they cut off your hands." He pulled the pack of Marlboros from his jeans pocket, tapping the box on the wood. "I guess it's like all the world's problems could be cured from cutting off the hands." He smashed a match across the pack, cupping his hand over the flame. There was another jolt of cold wind and he passed the cigarette to Rusty. "Couldn't steal, couldn't fist fight. Sure as shit couldn't shoot a gun. Hell, couldn't give somebody the finger."

"Couldn't jerk off."

"That's right."

The squeak-box-voice of a boy sounded off through the wind and Harlan glanced down the beach where a pack of kids were assembling a makeshift raft from driftwood and tire core.

Rusty watched them hurry into the shallow water.

A new wind swept from off the ocean, throwing sand and seaweed across the docks. Harlan wrapped his windbreaker over his head, huddling himself from the breeze.

"It's something to think about," Harlan said. "All those happy dolphins."

He tore out a page of his notebook and began to sketch the kids paddling out into the ocean. He changed his mind, crumpled the paper into a ball and threw it into the water. He said something about a life preserver.

Rusty laughed. He passed Harlan the joint.

❀❀❀

"The hell you doing?" Turco snatched the joint away and he pushed the boy against the alley wall. "You don't eat the shit! You smoke it."

The two boys were silent, tall for their age, thin as fence with faces that wore the first signs of acne. Dale knew Turco from Jess Holey at the sundries place. They had shoplifted together. He went to taste the marijuana again.

"What the Jesus Christ hell are you doing?" Turco barked. He threw back thick locks of bleach-blonde hair that covered his angular face and his eyes were blue wax paper that kept the boys at a nervous distance.

Eric, the one Turco had pushed, leaned against the alley wall. He twitched, plagued with some nervous tick and his hands, wet with sweat, rarely revealed themselves beyond his shorts pockets. An anxious grin swam around on his face and Turco had resented it the moment the three had met in the alley and he told them again how they were wasting his time.

Eric said, "Have to find out if it's krypto."

"Shut up."

"Dude."

"I said shut the fuck up."

Turco stood with the two boys in the alley between an arcade and a flower shop. The trash from the Gull's Nest Diner was clustered in the far corner and it stunk of rotted frozen fish dinners and from across the street, Turco could hear two girls whispering. They were clumped together like soda straws in matching reds and whites, huddling from the sharp cold. They had come with the boys to get the weed. They were afraid to look at Turco.

Nation Beach Winter Festival banners hung off the telephone poles, flapping in the strong winds and sunlight was everywhere, casting orbs of white over the metallic cars and trucks parked on the east side of the road. A closed sign flapped listlessly on a rusty chain before the Shell auto repair where Turco had once worked and he could make out its splintered windows from a tropical storm two months ago. The glass had not been replaced and his reflection showed countless forms of himself. Aside from George Caybe's Market one block down, all the stores were closed.

Turco pulled the joint from Dale's hand and held it into his face. "You think I'm riding you?"

"We don't know you," Eric said.

"Shut up." He pushed his finger into the small of Eric's chest. "Was I talking to you?"

Eric didn't answer, glancing down at his skateboard. The wind grew in force and it was cold.

"Was I fuckin talking to you?"

"No."

"Then shut up."

Turco ripped the bag out of Eric's hand, his lean arms hanging closely to his side. "What the fuck am I dealing with here? Who are you guys?"

The boys said nothing.

"You know me," Turco said. "You know who I am."

"Yeah, we know," Dale said.

"Then why you treatin' me like some kook from Fort Pierce?"

They looked at each other. Dale laughed.

"Stop flirting. Look at me, faggots."

Dale kicked a pebble away.

"Look at me."

They did, careful not to look directly into his eyes, shivering in the morning chill.

"This is grade-A ganga." Turco held the joint up to their faces. "Everglades-grown skunk." He pointed to the two girls. "You wanna squeeze those little titties?"

The girls turned away. The taller, sandy-haired girl with the headphones whispered something to her friend.

Turco turned back to the boys. He asked them if they wanted to touch some tits. Eric said they already had.

"Shit," Turco said, "those chicks will ball you inside-out once they smoke this."

Dale nodded and ran his hand over the smooth, wood surface of his skateboard. His face shined in the sunlight reflecting off the trash cans.

Turco watched the boy's eyes. They blinked nervously, bloodshot, weak from the sun. The boy rubbed his eyes and looked as though he'd fall against the wall. Turco put a hand on the boy's small shoulder. "Are you guys ready to be mature? You through with Romper Room?"

"We need a quarter," Dale said.

"A quarter."

"Yeah."

Turco fell quiet. "That's more like it."

He took a step back and eyed the street. The girls turned away.

He reached into his jeans crotch, making like he was adjusting his swim trunks. He gestured to the skateboard tucked underneath Eric's skinny arm. "You like those wheels?"

"They're all right."

"I don't get a good ride out'a those wheels." Turco pulled a zip-lock bag of marijuana from his crotch. "I like those new Peroltas."

He told them how he used to skate Main Street. He had used the bus bench as a platform and had nearly broken his leg trying to jump from roofs. He had fallen on the same trash cans that were now sitting in the alley, frosted over from the cold. He laughed and the boys laughed too and he mentioned again how much he liked the new Perolta wheels.

Dale smiled. "Yeah, I'm getting those Monday."

"Those are the shit." He kept the marijuana low to his side. "Those are good wheels."

A station wagon with North Carolina plates passed the intersection. It came to the corner where the two girls stood and they turned away from it, making for the bus stop and the car finally turned and rolled away and the street was quiet again. Turco engaged the boys and told them that it was a first-time deal and they'd be saving some money.

"Cool," Eric said.

"Thirty-five."

Eric stood silent for a moment, then pulled out the wad of dollar bills from his shorts pocket and handed Turco the cash.

Turco studied the ball of crumpled bills. "The hell is this?"

"What?"

"You got anything a little bigger than George Washington?"

Eric stood frozen. He nudged Dale. "Got anything, dude?"

"I only got nine singles."

Turco sighed. The breeze had suddenly become low and weaker; the lumbering, warped smoke cloud from the shuttle explosion now wore a bleak, gray film. Although still cold, Turco was sweating from his eyes and the boys saw this and began to cuss.

Turco told them to shut up. He snatched the dollar bills from Eric's hand, gesturing to the girls standing across the street. "Your chicks."

"Yeah?"

"Go ask your chicks. Girls always have money."

"All right, hang on." Dale slapped the board down, rolling it onto the street. Eric followed Dale, tripping mid-street, skinning his knee. They met up with the two girls and began to argue.

Standing alone, Turco pulled a pack of Marlboros from his pocket. He creaked his neck and stared into the sky. The shuttle explosion was bigger, fuller, appreciating westward. The smoke cloud bore no shapes he could immediately comprehend. They were tentacles more than anything; stretching, extending out for open space. A dead roach was smeared on the sidewalk and Turco watched ants parade around its body.

Another cold pass of wind came and he looked across to the two boys. They were cursing the girls. The one with the headphones had begun to shout back and she was ready to run off.

Turco told them to hurry up. His face was growing numb by the chilly breeze and he couldn't remember when it had been this cold.

Dale grabbed at the girl's purse and she screamed and she took her friend's hand and together they fled to the elementary school park a block away.

The girl was crying.

Turco lit his cigarette. He stared back into sky and watched the shuttle cloud.

❀❀❀

Exit 41A on the Florida Turnpike was a slim, tangled line of motionless vehicles and Grant kept his eyes to the till, occasionally glancing up to see the crawling traffic sound off in horns and engine exhaust.

A drab-green Volvo crept up to the toll booth, headlights lingering from the dawn drive. The driver, a lumpy-faced man with a tangled beard and small pocks for eyes, stuck his head out the window, handing Grant the ticket. He asked if he was at the exit to Kennedy.

"No, sir." Grant put the ticket through a slit in the wooden drawer and counted the rest of the till. Most of the bills had been singles, clumped together in the drawer, bound with rubber bands. A tiny alarm clock ticked slow, grating clicks and the sound was everywhere.

The driver of the Volvo said something under his breath and Grant could make out a large smear on his dashboard from spilled coffee. The windshield was stained with bits of flies and dry rain drops. Grant wondered how far the man had driven in the early morning.

The driver asked Grant where he was.

"Nation Beach, sir. You owe another dollar."

The driver stared at Grant. He fished out another dollar. "How do I get to Cape Kennedy?"

"You can't. Incoming's blocked."

"You're kidding."

Grant shook his head. "No, unfortunately, you're going to have to go back to Exit 27." He faced the man with bloodshot eyes. "Take Exit 27 to Candlelight."

"I have to get back on the goddamned state road?"

"Exit 41's shut down. You can't get nowhere today."

"Jesus Christ."

A motor trailer honked from behind. Two men had gotten out of their cars and begun to cuss at one another and a woman screamed for her husband to return to their truck.

Grant closed his till, preparing to leave. "Sir, you either have to pass through or turn back."

"I wanna speak to someone in charge."

Tim Parish, an elderly man with a small smile entered Grant's booth. The smell of his coffee filled the air. "Good shift, Grant?"

"Tired. This man needs to talk to Mike."

"Mike ain't here yet, he can talk to me." Tim patted Grant on the back. "You're out'a here."

"I am, Tim."

"Happy Birthday."

"Thanks." Grant opened the door and grabbed his Ron Jon's zip-up hanging on the booth's open window. The driver in the Volvo watched him walk away and he shouted at Grant to return to the toll booth and raise up the gate.

Grant passed the line of booths that separated the cars from the miles of beach town beyond Exit 41A. A cold sun beat down upon his head, warming his black hair and scalp. Crows circled the dusty sides of highway, searching for scraps that had fallen from the windows of passing cars and their caws echoed through the frosted orange groves.

Fumbling the buttons on his uniform, Grant set loose his tee shirt. Like his jeans, it wore the dull brown of a coffee stain.

His '73 Volkswagon Superbeetle was parked in the lot just off the Tourist Information Center. He had bought the car on finance and seven payments made before the engine had begun to rattle and the electrical system had given out. He'd stuck duct tape on the rear view mirror that was busted and a cop had given him a shitty time about the black tint. Climbing into the driver's seat, he turned the rearview on his face. The dashboard smelled of stale marijuana and Libby's lipstick.

He took a beach towel from the back and put it over his seat and started the ignition.

Horns sounded off from the congested turnpike and nothing moved.

Grant peeled onto the highway and took a utility path to St. Anne Road. It was a long, lonely snake of road that wound through the orange groves and back into town. More crows were lurking beneath the trees, pillaging rotten fruit. They took to the air in black paintbrush strokes, spooked by the burp and choke of the car's exhaust.

The VW's clutch was idling, hard to start from the cold, creating a crunching sound that soon became drowned in a blast of heavy Metallica.

Grant put the window down and the car was still hot. The smell of orange grove spread through the air and he rubbed sweat from his eyes. It was almost noon.

From her bedroom, Libby could hear Grant's Beetle rumbling through the gates of the Sun Gardens Mobile Community.

Running into the kitchen, feeding the sink Lemon Joy, she left the dishes to soak. Half the laundry was done and she could finish up her father's shirts before heading out to the party. Her supermarket uniform was still only half-buttoned and the nametag dangled on the crest and she ran back into the living room, checking her lipstick in the mirror.

"I'm gonna leave the dishes soaking, Dad. Use the paper plates."

Dan Nearly sat on the couch in boxer shorts and an old Marines tee shirt. His barrel build stuck through the tattered shirt like clusters of volcanic rock and his bad leg was up on a pillow. A paper towel filled with ice was wrapped around his knee.

"It's the damndest thing," he said and stared into the TV at the replaying video of the booster rocket discharging from the shuttle's fuselage.

Libby asked him if he had heard her.

Dan nodded, keeping his stare fixed to the TV. "I gotta use the paper plates?"

"They're in the left-side cabinet."

"All right, honey."

She told him she'd return later to wash the rest of his shirts. Maybe they'd get a bite to eat before he left for work.

"That sounds fine, Libby."

The VW's engine roared beyond the trailer home's walls. It rattled the sink water. The dog was barking, tearing at the fence.

"There's your ride," Dan hollered.

Libby searched through the clutter of used magazines and want-ads on the small coffee table. "You see my keys 'round?"

A horn sounded off over the engine rattle.

"You check your bedroom?"

"Yeah." She swore under her breath and suddenly spotted the keys on the couch's cushion beside her father. "Lord, gimme eyes." She scooped up the keys, buttoning the rest of her uniform. There was a small, electrical heater in the corner, filling the room with heat but it was still cold. "You want me to bring anything back?"

"Coffee."

"We need coffee?"

Dan nodded.

"All right."

"Might pop in later, say hi."

"Okay, Dad." She kissed him good-bye. "Stop in."

Most likely, he wouldn't. He had an appointment with that doctor at the VA. They'd make him wait an extra hour and he had claims to file. From there, he'd only have a half hour or so before his shift at the liquor store. The manager had warned him of being late again and she worried he'd lose his job.

She told Dan she loved him and no worries if he couldn't drop by. She rushed out the door before Dan could ask her to shut the space heater off.

Leaning out of the VW, Libby gazed out to the traffic running north out of town. She had seen it only once this bad. Hurricane David. A coastal-wide evacuation. She and her father had fled to the inland and they were stuck on the side of a rest area ten miles outside Orlando and she remembered gazing into the storm, trying to see through it. When the rain had turned ugly, they took shelter in a highway vending station. Her father had bought her a Snickers bar and a soda and she was shaking, cold from the storm. Gusts of wind had found their way into the station's vents, pelting their faces with rain. Her father had told her silly jokes and Marine stories.

He held her in his arms and she fell asleep and dreamed.

Grant turned his eyes from the road, adjusting the radio for reports on the Challenger. Libby saw the broken bits of red in his eyes and could tell that he hadn't slept. The double shifts made him drowsy, irritable. It wasn't healthy. Seeing his eyes red in the morning sunlight, she felt like saying something. She resisted, wiping a tinge of lipstick from her mouth. She held her hands to the car's heater and asked Grant if he could turn off the radio.

"Why?"

"I've been crying about it for the last hour. Could you just please turn it off?"

Grant turned off the radio and put a Circle Jerks tape into the cassette player. Distortion filled the car and a voice screamed about a gun.

"Can't believe how cold it is," Libby said.

"29 degrees last night."

"I believe it, nearly froze under the sheets." Libby then asked him if he had cigarettes.

Grant gestured to the dashboard at the pack of Marlboros.

"First I can't find my keys, now I forget the cigs."

"You lost your keys?"

"No. Almost lost em, but I totally forgot my cigs."

"Forget anything else?"

She faced him and smiled. "Hush. Didn't forget your birthday." She reached over, kissing his cheek. "Got your present ready for tonight. My baby's nineteen."

She lit the cigarette.

"A hundred and sixty thousand."

"What's that?"

"Hours. 160 thousand hours old. And change."

Libby thought about that and the numbers impressed her and she smiled. "It's a lot when you say it like that."

The Winn-Dixie supermarket was a featureless, red and brown cinderblock whose parking lot was overflowing. Cars sat in sprawling lines, waiting out the next available spaces and the outpour bled onto Federal Highway and police were beginning to force drivers back around.

Libby could hear the voice of store manager Burt Frosta shouting across the intercom for additional help on the speed lanes. The main sliding doors weren't functioning and winos from the Big-Daddy's tavern were huddled around a small trash fire.

Grant pulled up before the loading zone. He followed behind Libby as she made her way towards the supermarket. A rolling shopping cart swept past them and Grant stopped it from crashing into a small Dautsun that was backing out.

"You getting off at nine?" he asked, counting a few dollars from his pocket.

"Nine-thirty."

Grant asked Libby if they were still going to Todd Hailer's party.

"I dunno. His girl gonna be there?"

"Lea? Yeah, I'm almost positive."

"She's got that laugh." Libby zipped closed her purse. "Giddy little laugh."

Grant spotted Harlan bucking back and forth on the coin-op Rocket Thunder ride at the front entrance.

Libby asked Harlan if he was having fun.

"Yeah. You got another quarter?"

Children in fat winter jackets clung to shopping carts, watching Harlan from inside the store.

The rocket buzzed and rattled and then came to a dead stop and Harlan struggled out the tiny cockpit.

Libby leaned in to Grant. "Stop in and see me later?"

"Yeah."

"Promise?"

"Yeah."

"Say I promise."

He looked at her and she smiled and whispered something and she kissed his face and it was soft and slow and warmed his cold skin. She pulled her purse over her shoulder and smiled once more. "See ya soon." She waved and slipped through the doors.

Harlan turned around and gestured to the traffic in the parking lot. "You believe this?"

"Crazy, right?" Grant checked his pack of Marlboros. There were a couple of cigarettes left.

Harlan asked if the turnpike was a mess.

"Two miles down," Grant answered. "Bumper to bumper. I need cigs."

"They raised the prices. Dollar more."

"You're kidding."

Harlan motioned to one of the checkouts where employees were cracking open boxes of cigarettes and batteries. "They're hikin everything up."

Grant glanced into the store. The customer lines wound their way around to the deli and produce departments. A black girl, screaming, fell into a puddle of water made from the broken-down ice machine and more water was beginning to creep across the store's linoleum.

"It's a space shuttle," Grant said, "not World War Three."

"Try telling them that." Harlan spat and pointed to the crowds of shoppers. "People think some kind'a fallout's gonna happen from the exhaust chemicals and shit. Everybody's scrambling." He lit the last of Grant's cigarettes. He threw the crumpled pack at the rocket ride that twin brothers shared. "Meteorites!"

The twins giggled. They screamed for more.

12:14 P.M.

They were on the highway and it looked bad and Grant turned left on Dover in the hopes of clearing the heavy traffic. "You see that thing fire up?"

"Shit, man," Harlan said, rolling the window down, "I was sitting on the rocks when it fireball. Scary as shit."

Harlan breathed in the cold ocean air, taking in the residential streets around them. Small cubes of beachside homes. Wooden road barriers had been put along the sidewalks and a couple of National Guardsmen dressed in camouflage sat in a jeep and more road barriers were stacked in the back of the jeep. Some of the local kids had used them as bike ramps.

Harlan was still stoned from earlier at the dock, his skin numb. He realized he smelled of Coppertone and cigarettes. He turned back to Grant and wished him Happy Birthday.

"Don't remind me," Grant mumbled.

"Big 19, last of the teens. Wrote a little something in the spirit of the occasion."

"Dirty?"

Harlan smiled and looked down at his spiral notebook. He asked Grant if he wanted it to be.

"Naw, guess not."

"Well, it ain't."

"So let's hear it."

"It's not ready."

"Oh yeah? Gotta wait for this thing?"

"This stuff takes time."

Grant faced him and grinned. "Since when your poems take time?"

Harlan smiled. "This one's different."

"You're startin to take em pretty seriously, huh."

"I dunno, I like it."

"Poetry?"

"Writing, I guess."

They reached the pier before one. Out-of-town plates crowded the sides of A1A and more police and another army jeep was parked before the pier entrance and soldiers with guns stood at the ticket booth. From the parking lot to the fringe of beach, people stood on the hoods and roofs of their vehicles, binoculars pointed at the distant Kennedy launch peninsula. Dogs roamed the parking lot, freed of leashes, chasing gulls.

Four launch pillars stood a quarter mile apart from one another. Their beacons were slow and reminded Harlan of lighthouses that sat at the edge of rocks and stared into cold, northeastern seas.

Grant studied the pier. Like the parking lot, it was badly overcrowded; its sides lathered with locals and tourists. People took photos and threw breadcrumbs into the water where pelicans begged and there was still some frost on the windshields of cars.

Grant lit a cigarette. He told Harlan he hadn't slept in twenty four hours.

"We gotta get this shit over with."

Harlan spat and motioned to the far end of the pier. "Turco's hanging with the fishermen."

"He better be ready," Grant said. "The guy likes to piss around."

12:51 P.M.

Turco pinched the exotic metal and turned the necklace over. It was a pale gold, rusted. Not like the necklace he had imagined. He wasn't sure it was real. He told Mars Bohr it was fading.

"The hell it is."

Mars peeled open a pack of Twinkies, biting the head off one of the cakes. Bits of it became caught in his black beard and his face was red charcoal from bad time spent under the Florida sun.

Fisherman stood behind them and cussed the growing packs of tourists on the pier and Turco wished they'd have done this kind of business somewhere else, perhaps in the parking lot or maybe the iHop on Federal Highway. He examined the necklace again. He shook his head, digging into his jeans pocket. "I don't know, it feels tarnished."

Mars Bohr snatched back the chain and held it out in front of Turco's face. "This is coated in Zeneclore. You know what that shit is?"

Turco pulled a cigarette from his pack.

"It's the stuff they put on the space shuttle. Keeps it from going too hot when it jams back into the atmosphere."

"Goddamn shuttle exploded," Turco said, cradling himself from the chilly breeze. "I don't want this shit exploding."

Mars Bohr mumbled something and scratched his beard. More bits of Twinkie scattered and he shook his head and tucked the necklace back into his parka. "Go to the Swap Shop fer all I care. But brother, this is the best deal you're gonna get on gold."

Turco lit his cigarette and more ocean wind stirred off the end of the pier, blowing back his tangle of blond dreadlocks. He studied Bohr's leathery face and asked to see the necklace again.

Bohr handed it back.

Turco studied the small engravings that twisted across the metal's strip. Pale, winter sunlight glistened off its edges. "What is all this shit anyway?"

"Mayan," Bohr said. "Know anything about em?"

"Mexicans, right?"

"A lot more than that."

Turco took a drag of his cigarette. The sun beat on his face and his lips were chapped. A stingray rash across his thigh had begun to itch and he asked Bohr how much.

"What'd you think we said?"

"I think we said fifty."

"Then that's what we said."

Turco killed his cigarette. He pulled two twenties and two fives from his pocket, making a point to stuff the bills into Mars' palm.

"That's gonna make a nice birthday gift," Mars said. He counted the bills one over the next.

Turco scratched the stingray rash. He cursed under his breath. "Just remember, I could'a gone to Temba's brother."

"Yeah," Bohr groaned. He stuffed the money into the pocket of his beach shorts, giving Turco a fast salute and disappeared into the crowds of tourists.

Alone, Turco studied the boardwalk. Some of the fisherman were reeling their lines in, starting to pack it in. The morning's catches were a general disappointment.

He had often fished with his brother when he was young. He had helped his brother reel in catches and the memory clung to him each time he found himself at the end of the pier. There were times when he was a boy and the fish were bigger than anything he had ever seen. His brother had always laughed when the fish fought the line.

From the pier's vantage, he could make out the swarm of activity at the launch pillars. Government vehicles rushed back and forth over the tarmacs that were now off-limits to civilian traffic. The cloud of rocket smoke was still dense and splitting out like a broken clover and as white as a sun's flare. Turco wondered if it would ever begin to fade. A ripple of jet engine erupted from F-15s overhead and the fishermen cussed. There was sun but it was still cold and the fishermen swore about the cold, too.

Gordey's hotdog stand sat at the south end of the pier. Turco found the grill closed. A hand-written note posted on the door said something about the shuttle explosion and that the restaurant would reopen later that afternoon. From the vending machine, he bought a pack of sunflower seeds and a can of orange soda. He fed seeds to a pelican that was perched on the pier railing, its feathers ruffled from the cold.

He took another look at the gold necklace.

The Mayan influence made him think of jungles. His father had told him and his brother stories of the Amazon and the waterfalls; enormous kingdoms, primal and ancient. His father had been an assistant contractor or engineer or something connected to the building of irrigation plants and when he drank he told them stories about the jungles.

The soda had made him want to take a piss and he started off to the restroom. He turned a corner and a voice called out from the crowd: "There he is, officer."

Turco snapped around, on alert, but it was only Harlan and he was smiling and making his way through the crowd with Grant.

Turco tucked the necklace away into his jeans pocket and pulled his pack of cigarettes.

"You blow up that shuttle?" Grant asked.

Turco grinned. "Shit, man, you see that?" Turco pointed into the sky. Vapor trail slashed through the blue. "Fucker blew up in like, five parts."

"More like eight."

"I gotta get a piece of that shuttle." Turco fought the wind and lit a new cigarette. "Shit's all kinds'a worth something."

"What's been going on here?"

"Bullshit." Turco gestured to the crowds in the parking lot. "Been getting worse every passing goddamn minute." He snuck a drag of his cigarette and shook his head. "Can't tell you how many news vans I've already seen."

They walked back to the front of the pier. More crowds hugged the railing and took photos of the smoke cloud. An elderly couple from England asked Turco if he could take their photo with the smoke cloud in the background. When he did, they thanked him and asked how far Disney Land was.

"It's pretty far," Turco said, pointing out to the ocean. "Disney Land's in California. We got Disney World." He told them it was three hours inland but there was no way they'd get within an inch of it by the afternoon. They thanked him again and headed off to take more photos.

Grant didn't ask Turco about the favor until they were in the parking lot. "Where is this place?"

"Delilia Plaza, off Dixie," Turco said.

"Shit," Grant mumbled, climbing into his car, "I need some sleep." He lit a cigarette from the new pack and cranked the ignition.

It wasn't until they were back on A1A that Turco rolled the joint. He was a quick roller and Harlan admired how efficiently he tucked the grains of pot into the paper. He made a hump that was just wide enough to stave off a fast burn and keep the marijuana contained.

Black Flag blasted on the stereo.

Turco could hear Harlan in the back seat, saying something about a concert in Orlando. He sealed the joint with a lick and told Harlan that he didn't like the band.

"They're kind'a good, I just think they have a weird singer."

"I know her," Turco said. "She's a bitch, she calls herself Black Janet." He told Harlan her real name was Claire and she was from Jacksonville and her brother used to sell dope on the pier with Turco and that he was an asshole.

Turco passed the joint to Harlan, who sat ready with a lighter. The car's engine rattled and bucked.

Grant concentrated on the traffic. The intersection was blocked both ways by local enforcement patrols and Nation Beach police had called on county support and everywhere Grant looked, there were state troopers with radios. They wore sunglasses and their uniforms were starched, straight as perfect lines.

Grant told Turco to lower the joint.

"Screw 'em, they're all busy with this shit."

Harlan went to light the joint.

"Harlan, I'm serious," Grant said. "Put down the goddamn joint."

Harlan hesitated, glancing at Turco. He put the joint down as they passed the police cars. He had burned his thumb from the lighter but kept quiet about it.

A state trooper was giving a man in a Trailblazer a ticket. His children sat restless in the back seats. Turco waved and a little girl saw Turco and waved back and her two brothers pointed to the lines of cars that were waiting inspection.

After crossing the intersection, Turco told Harlan to light the joint.

"No," Grant said.

"Grant, what the hell, man?"

"Just wait a goddamn second, Turco."

"Roll up the windows, you got hardcore tint."

Harlan leaned into the front seats. His thumb was now red from the burn. He asked them if he was lighting the joint.

"Yes."

"No."

"Grant, Jesus."

"Where'd you get that shit anyway?" Grant asked.

Turco paused. "What do you mean, where'd I get it? I sell it for chrissakes."

"I saw Vay yesterday."

Turco rolled down his window and spat into the street. He watched the police-patrolled intersection slip away behind them. He told Harlan to give him the joint.

"Turco."

"Yeah."

"I saw Vay yesterday," Grant said again.

"So what."

"He was wondering where you were."

Turco struggled with Harlan's lighter, sparking the joint in two thumb rolls. He cussed out the lighter.

"He was looking for you," Grant said.

Turco took a hit of the joint and told Grant to turn onto Crosby.

"He says you owe him money."

The marijuana was harsh. Turco coughed and swore and passed the joint back to Harlan.

"Is that his dope you're smoking?" Grant asked.

"Shut up already, Grant."

"How much you owe him?"

"Nothing, don't worry about it." He opened the glove compartment and began to riffle through Grant's cassette tapes.

"He says you owe about fifteen hundred."

"Fifteen hundred?" Harlan blew smoke out his nose and mouth and he coughed and rubbed his eyes.

Turco pulled out a cassette from the stereo, feeding a new tape into the slit. It was Talking Heads and he turned the stereo up.

"You owe Vay fifteen hundred," Grant said. "You're not worried about that."

"Half the money's mine."

"You gonna pay him that money?"

"Grant, is this a problem for you?"

"Look, man-"

"No, dude, you look." His voice rose. "It's not your cross to bear. Maybe if Vay would chill out for two seconds, I could find a few bucks lying around."

"He was pissed."

"He can go to hell. He's lucky I'm not taking the shit and selling it down in Sebastian." He pointed to the distant rows of aluminum-sided beach homes and the ocean beyond their fences. "I can work this beach like nobody else. Until I get some respect, Vay's not getting jack-shit." He rolled down the window and marijuana was sucked into the cold air. "Besides, I can make it up on the next score."

The Beetle braked before a new intersection on Palmory. A red Volkswagon Cabriolet pulled up beside them at the light. Two blonds and a brunette filled the car. They looked around sixteen, dressed in tanktops, wearing sunglasses as if defying the cold. The brunette sat in the back, staring down at a map and New Order poured through the car windows.

Turco told Grant to roll the windows down and he shouted to them. He asked if they were from Orlando and the blond in the passenger's seat began to grin. He shouted the question again.

She shouted back that they were from West Palm.

"That's far."

The blond giggled and leaned into her friend's ear and Turco could make out her right nipple, half-exposed through her loose bikini top.

The light turned green and both cars started out.

Turco nudged Grant to slow down.

The blond in the passenger's seat screamed back to Turco: "How far's Cape Canaveral from here?"

"Why the hell you wanna go there?"

"We came to see the shuttle!" The brunette's hair-sprayed curls poured over her face.

"Shuttle? It blew up."

"We know!"

The girl driving kept silent. She had a lean face, half-covered by cinnamon-brown hair and baby shoelaces were tied to her wrists.

The brunette threw the road map to the floor and stuck her head out the car window. She shouted if they had any weed.

Turco nodded and he shouted back that they had weed.

The lanes grew farther apart and the cars separated through a highway divider.

Turco stuck his head back out the window, shouting to them: "Meet us at Nation pier in an hour!"

"Nation pier?"

"Yeah!"

"All right, bye!"

Turco rolled up the window, picking the joint out of Harlan's fingers.

"That was a nice Cabriolet they were driving," Harlan said.

"Daddy bought it at Toys-R-Us," Turco said. He watched the car disappear through an intersection.

❦❦❦

The medical supply store was in a strip mall, squashed between an Eckerd's Drugs and a Little Caesar's pizza restaurant.

Turco was the first to walk through the door. The smell was musty, fermented. Dust particles floated in the cold trappings of sunlight and the windows appeared endlessly glossed.

Harlan went to the wheelchairs that sat clumped together in the corner.

Grant followed Turco up to the counter where a middle-aged black man with a maroon tie was drinking coffee. A small television sat on the counter, glowing news and the counter was littered with cigarette butts from an overflowing ashtray.

Turco explained to the man about the respirator motor and why it wasn't functioning.

The man sat his cigarette on the end of the overflowing ashtray and asked Turco questions. The man checked a policy number from a file cabinet beside the register. He asked Turco what his brother's name was.

"Turcorelli. First name, Lucas."

The man went through the file cabinet as though he'd done it a thousand times. His thumbs were covered in cigarette resin. The man pulled out a worn manila folder and asked Turco if he had an insurance card.

"No, I ordered the thing three weeks ago. Should be cleared."

The man looked over the folder of Lucas Turcorelli. He shook his head. "Expired."

"What?"

"That insurance has expired."

Turco glanced over the file. It was filled with thick paragraphs and he found the date the manager had been pointing to and asked if it was expired.

"That's what I said."

"The-"

"American Mobility, yes."

Harlan played in a motorized wheelchair. The sound of rotors whined through the store.

The man snapped up his cigarette and took a drag. He asked Turco if he was Wayne Turcorelli.

"No. He's not around."

"Who are you?"

"Brian. I'm his son. And that policy insures my brother."

"This policy's been void for the last four months. On top'a that, you gotta be eighteen to claim any medical equipment." The man coughed. His teeth, chalk yellow, showed brightly through his black skin. He asked Turco if he was eighteen.

Turco wiped a new film of sweat from his forehead. Although it was unseasonably cold, the air of the store felt thick and warm and the oscillating fan on the counter did little to spread it around. Static buzzed on the TV.

"Look," Turco said, "I need that part."

The man shook his head, smashing his burning cigarette into the thick of the ashtray. "I'm sorry. I can't give you that part." He lit another cigarette, pointing at Harlan who was spinning wheelies in the chair. "Son, you need to stop doing that."

On television, a vapor trail splattered the sky. Peter Jennings spoke and the news report cut to a commercial for skin cream.

"You can call American Moe," the man said, "but they're gonna tell you the same thing-"

Turco smashed his hand against the counter. The motion was abrupt and ugly and the man took a step back and pulled the cigarette from his lips.

Turco looked back at the store manager who was still silent. He told the man his brother needed the motor for the respirator. "It won't function right without it."

"I understand that, but I can not-"

"Goddamn it!" Turco said it again, loud enough that Harlan had stopped playing with the wheelchair. "Will you just help me out here? Will you gimme a break?!"

The man slipped his cigarette back between his lips, taking the file and placing it back in the cabinet. His hands were shaking. His wrists, black and arthritic, filled with spots and veins, seemed detached from the rest of his body. He slammed shut the file. He calmed himself and told Turco he couldn't do anything until he got a hold of the prime medical provider.

"No," Turco said, "there is something you can do."

"Sir."

"He needs that part."

The man held out his hand. "Sir."

"What."

"Sir?"

"What?!"

The man gave a wheezing breath and his hands were still shaking. "If you don't control yourself, I'm gonna call the police."

"Oh, fuck you, man."

"This has been a bad morning and you're making it worse."

"No, you're the one making this worse."

The man rubbed his eyes, gesturing to a lime-green phone which sat at the end of the counter. "I'm calling the police."

"Call em," Turco said.

The man mumbled his wife's name and started to the phone.

Grant approached the counter. Like Turco, he was sweating from the store's dry heat and his hair had begun to wet. "Turco."

"I'm calling them," the man muttered.

"Goddamn call them."

"Turco," Grant whispered again. "Let's just go."

Grant put a hand on his shoulder and Turco flinched and pushed Grant's hand away.

Harlan was now out of the wheelchair and watching the commotion.

The man picked up the phone receiver and began stabbing buttons. He told Turco that he was calling the police.

"Yeah, I know. You said that already."

"I'll say it again then."

"I don't care."

"I want you out of my store."

"I know you do."

The man's face had filled with sweat. His hands shook and he gestured to the TV. "You see this? You see what the hell happened to our country today? I don't need to deal with this today." He turned back to Turco, a faint drum in his voice. "Don't need to deal with any'a this shit today."

"Yeah so call the cops. C'mon."

"This is where you walk away."

"No."

"You need to walk away."

"I'm not going anywhere."

The man stood cold. He hung up the phone. He looked at Turco. "Just leave, all right?"

"No."

"You need to leave."

"No."

"Please," he said. "Please leave." His voice was weak and his breath stunk of cigarettes.

"How much is the motor?"

The man turned off the television. He rubbed his eyes. Again he asked Turco to leave.

"How much is the goddamn motor?"

The man swallowed a piece of cigarette tobacco. "Fourteen hundred."

"Fourteen hundred."

"Yes, sir."

They drove across the street to the Flagler bank with the ATM. Turco had had trouble with the machine before and he smashed the screen with the palm of his hand and the buttons, slick from sweat, caused him to cancel his transaction. He jammed his card into the slot and began again. He drew some attention from a guard and the small line of cars that crept through the bank's drive-thru.

The station wagon with the Carolina plates had driven into the lot and a man ran into the bank with car keys rattling.

Grant stood beside Turco at the ATM machine. He asked him what he was doing.

"The shit keeps canceling." Turco tapped in his code. A new screen showed 1550.00.

"That's Vay's money," Grant said.

"No. It's in my account. It's my money."

He punched another key. The ATM churned and flipped and spat out money. He pulled the maximum five hundred dollars and repeated the process.

Grant scratched his scalp. He had an impulse to get in the car and drive away. Leave Turco at the bank and go home and sleep. He was standing in the middle of a parking lot next to an ATM machine. He felt the cold around him and there was no wind. He looked back at Turco, his eyes bloodshot from no sleep. "You've been taking money from Vay?"

"Piss on Vay," Turco barked. "This is my money. Made it on my scores."

"By selling his shit."

Harlan overheard them, flinching as a tractor trailer blew by on the highway and he moved closer to the ATM. "That's Vay's money, Turco?"

Turco didn't answer. He pressed a green button and another five hundred slid out.

The traffic on Dixie had merged into a fine, thin line of vehicles that flowed into State Street and Harlan counted the number of television vans. Some he had recognized from local news stations. Others were from as far as Miami and Atlanta and there was a food truck parked off the side of Dixie, serving a steady flow of construction workers and news people and Harlan could smell the burning salt of soft pretzels and charbroiled hot dogs.

Turco sat silent in the passenger's seat, the respirator motor packaged in a small box on his lap. Like Harlan, he stared out to the food service truck and the crowds that grew around it. The opposing traffic was pushing northward from Nation Beach and he was beginning to see clearer road.

In the last hour, his eyes had become dry and his face felt coarse and weighted down, as though it had been slept on. The churning roar of traffic that had once seemed organized and flowing, like pipe organs of a carousel ride, had turned stale and horns sounded off from different directions. They passed the marina and the stench of boat diesel filled the air.

Driving over the causeway, he could see the long sets of waves from Kemper Point. They pounded the shoreline, taking the curved shape of the cove. Pelicans duck-dived for fluke and Harlan studied an elderly bird with black marks over its back. Local kids had tried to tar it and it had survived. It swam alone to itself, arthritic, indifferent. It lingered in the deep water, bobbing around the ebb and flow of the outside break.

"Tide's closing out soon," Harlan said, motioning to the distant waves. "We getting wet or what?"

Grant said nothing, rolling open the window and throwing his cigarette into the wind. An air freshener tied to the rearview mirror began to spin and flicker.

"Smoke a couple'a jays," Harlan said. "Get some waves, that's what I'm talking about."

"That was stupid, Turk," Grant said.

Turco told him to piss off.

"Vay needs that money and you goddamn-"

"Fuck Vay!" Turco kicked the dashboard, causing the frame to rattle.

Harlan stopped moving his head to the thump of base blasting from the back speakers and he saw that Turco's foot had made an imprint in the dashboard.

Turco took a small breath. "What am I supposed to do, Grant? Leave my brother sitting in the corner of our living room, breathing into a goddamn paper bag?!"

"The guy at the store was right. You could'a checked the insurance."

"Yeah, right."

"No! You could'a checked the-"

"Bullshit! It was canceled!"

The car fell silent. Grant lowered the volume on the tape deck, finally turning the stereo off and rolling open a window. Wind crept into the VW's interior, blowing across Turco's face. Loose strands of dreadlock, bleached from sun, fell into his eyes and he brushed them away.

Grant swallowed a breath, glancing at Turco's foot imprint, now fading on the cracked dashboard. "You know for a fact it was canceled?"

Turco nodded. He mumbled something about his father. "Asshole thought we'd be able to trace him through his policy."

Turco rolled his window down and gazed at the vacant shops on Main Street. Closed signs hung on the doors and the alley where he had sold dope was now filled with more trash. There was a box of broken glass and some discarded paint cans. The remainder of its contents was spilled over onto the sidewalk and there was a damaged porch door thrown to the side.

The day his father had left.

He went to get something at work and he'd be back to fix the backyard screen and they would work together to repair the siding and he had told Turco to wait for him at the house.

Hurricane shutters hung over the store windows and bright sunlight reflected off the metal and into Turco's face.

❦❦❦

The house was weathered, wind-beaten like most on the block. Mary Turcorelli had gotten the estimate on the roof. The man from the Titusville Sears wouldn't be able to start the work before mid-February and until then, she'd have to endure the rain leaks. Her neighbor had just replaced her roof and pool screens and the price was more than she could afford and if another bad rain were to hit in the coming summer, the roof probably wouldn't hold. The man had told her he was absolutely sure of that and that he'd also need to most likely replace her backyard screens. She had thanked him for the estimate. He was nice enough and told her that if she changed her mind, he could probably do it for a fair price.

She would think about it.

Since November, the weather had been generally bad. The recent cold snap was particularly cruel and she'd hope they'd sail through February before the March winds could intensify. They had endured the last storm. Turco was good with the makeshift panels and sealing duct tape over the glass. Mary believed that if he could do the same for the smaller parts of the ceiling, they might have a chance doing without the new roof.

She lit another cigarette and her mind ran from coffee. The replaying shuttle footage had been running all afternoon. The roof estimate was still in her hand; yellow, crinkled tissue paper. She set it down on the kitchen counter and turned the television off.

Turco sat crouched before the wheelchair, installation manual spread out before him. The manual was divided into three folding sections with English, Spanish and what Turco guessed was French. Sweat fell onto the open manual, blurring the words. His mother had dropped cigarette ashes onto the manual and when Turco wiped it off, an ugly, tar-colored smear was left behind. His hair had begun to cause him trouble and he'd twist and pull the tangle of dreadlocks from his face, concentrating on the respirator's illustrations.

"Do you have their number?" Mary asked again, trading a fresh cigarette. She repeated the question and Turco sighed. She watched him click another piece of the plastic tubing together. "Maybe they're in the Yellow Pages."

Turco kept quiet, fastening a tube onto the respirator's rotary motor.

His brother Lucas, twitching in the wheelchair, smiled frail and clumsily, gazing through the half-open patio door. He could see Grant and Harlan in the backyard, applying wax to the two short boards that sat in the weeds. He had counted three boards, including Turco's that was propped up on the side of the shed and he smiled again when he mumbled the number three. He had finished his orange juice and the straw was still dangling from his lower lip. He laughed and pulled it out of his mouth and set it on his lap. From the backyard, Harlan waved at him and he waved back.

Turco cursed. He cut his finger in between the respirator tube and the cylinder locket. He muttered something again, going back to the manual.

"What did you say?" Mary asked.

"I said shit."

"Maybe they're in the Yellow Pages."

"I don't know."

"You don't know what?" Mary brushed away hair strands from her eyes. "You don't know if they have the number?"

"It's not gonna matter."

"The policy was in both our names."

"Yeah, well," Turco said, "it don't look that way."

Mary paused. She put a cigarette to her lips and rinsed her hair into a bun. She walked into the kitchen. Magnets and coupons covered the refrigerator. Lucas began to make noise and Mary told him to hush up. He had stained his shirt from the orange juice and was pointing to it.

"I know, honey," Mary said, "I'm gonna clean it up. Just sit still so your brother can finish his stuff."

Turco told her it didn't matter but Mary ignored him and continued searching for the phone number. "All right," she finally screamed, throwing stacks of bills off the counter, "where's the Yellow Pages?"

"Mom, it's not gonna matter!"

"How can a father cancel an insurance policy on his own son, for chrissakes?!" She threw around papers, pizza menus, searching for the Yellow Pages. She fought open a cabinet, kicking it open and throwing trash bags and a flashlight onto the kitchen floor and Lucas cried about the orange juice and Mary crouched to the bottom cabinet and began to sort through the cleaners and disinfectants. She found the Yellow Pages in the rear of the cabinet, half-rotted from the leaking sink pipe.

Turco inserted a final screw into the motor's ventricle tube. He wore a grin that made his little brother laugh and clap his hands. "Let's see what we got here, Lucas."

Lucas laughed again. The voice pleased him and he reached out to touch Turco.

Turco tried the motor and the machine whined to life.

The respirator tube was attached to his brother's mouthpiece. It made a squeak, followed by a steady stream of air and then a long whisper from the respirator. Lucas talked to it. He clapped his hands when the whispering stopped.

Turco smiled. He nodded and said: "There it goes."

He took Lucas' hand and put it on the orange juice stain. Lucas laughed.

Standing in the muddy corner of the backyard, Harlan aimed the BB gun into the sky. The two crows Turco had shot down Sunday were still rotting on the other side of the fence. The smell was a mildew stench that made him think of dirty laundry and wet sandboxes.

Grant sat on his surfboard, drinking a warm beer beside the rusted, crumbling barbeque grill. The headache had returned. He took small sips of beer, washing it back and forth in his mouth. The pain coursed though his teeth, bringing pressure to his eyes. He had the urge to bite down hard and grind his teeth. He spat beer, inhaling a deep breath of afternoon air. He tried to find new traces of the shuttle explosion, but the whole image was beginning to recede and he knew that in a few hours, he'd barely be able to see it at all.

Harlan's beer sat on one of the patio chairs, unopened, warming in the sun. He aimed the BB gun at the rooster weather vane that sat on top the neighboring home and fired the gun. The sound of bullet stray was lost in wind chimes from the back porch.

The afternoon sky, once a vast cobalt blue, had since turned gray. Cold sunlight struggled to break and the wind was concentrated and fast. The weather vein circled like a spinning top, relentless, as if enough motion might propel it upwards and free it of the roof.

Turco came out the patio door into the yard, bare-chested, wearing surf shorts. He crouched down, covering his hands from the wind and lit a marijuana roach. His smaller surfboard was set on two cement bricks, covered in dirty beach towels. He threw off the towels, exposing the board. It was airbrushed in big tones of purple and red.

"Wind's kicking up," Turco said. "Cold bitch-of-a-day." He took another glance at the sky, arching his neck. He walked over to a barrel beside the porch door and pulled out a wetsuit. The material was soft foam and nylon and it melted through his fingers. He slipped one leg into the wetsuit, watching Harlan hold the BB gun. He told him he wasn't aiming right.

"I don't care."

"I could be ass-backwards-stoned," Turco said, "and I'd hit those crows."

Slipping into the wetsuit, Turco took a quick look at himself in the glass reflection of the patio door. He turned around to Grant, who had since finished his beer and was now watching the shuttle cloud. "Grant, you remember when I shot that hawk in Hobe Sound?"

Grant didn't answer. He closed his eyes, enduring a new wave of headache pain. Harlan asked him if he was okay. Grant nodded and fumbled for the surfboard, caught between a lawn mower and a portable generator.

Staring into sky, Turco zipped up his wetsuit, gesturing to the banyan tree hanging over the neighboring fence. "I shot that bitch right out'a the tree."

Harlan told him he was full of shit and Turco turned to Grant and pumped the BB gun. "Did I not shoot that bitch right out'a the tree?"

Grant looked between the slants of wooden fence at a neighbor's pool. It was green and dirty and a plastic float glided on the water's surface. One of the crows had swooped down onto the pool's edge and was cleaning its wings.

Grant watched the bird caw and fly off into the sky.

Turco picked up the BB rifle and aimed it into sun. "Check this out."

He held his breath, pulling the trigger. He shot the crow and it dropped from the sky, falling, fluttering like a black oil rag to earth.

❦❦❦

Monster Hole was named for the schools of thresher sharks that migrated through the south channels every winter. Turco had spotted a couple off the pier. They swerved through the bait lines, mechanical and graceless. From the shore, their dorsal fins were tiny pine saws, disorganized and splintered, moving in every direction.

Harlan too, had spotted the small pack when they first arrived at the beach. There was a new, northerly breeze that swarmed across the jetty, blowing sand around in tiny spirals. Harlan had caught a bit of Rusty Vay's cold and changed his mind about surfing, choosing instead to sit on the beach and watch over Grant and Turco's belongings. He found a low-sunken dune that shielded him from the wind and lit a joint. His notebook, half-filled with writing and sketches, sat beside him in the sand.

Slick, wet-suited forms of surfers filled the water like colored kites in a dark storm. The currents shifted them around the outside break, pushing them closer to the rock jetty that struck out into the water.

Devlin Hall, a dealer Turco knew from Cocoa City, missed a sharp cutback and crashed into the surge.

Turco saw it and grinned. "Devlin. That asshole couldn't catch air in a goddamn oxygen tank." He spat out the last of a marijuana roach he had been chewing. He laughed and shouted out to Devlin.

Grant rubbed sex wax over his board. He stared out past the first line of surfers to the far break where old-timers sat on their longboards. They were pointing to the cloud of chemicals that had expanded upon the blue sky like white spackle.

"Who's out there?" Turco asked, putting a hand over his eyes to deflect the sun. "Will Betters, Dusty?"

Grant pointed to a skinhead diving off the edge of the jetty. "There's Sean."

"Christ, is that Sean?" Turco asked.

"Yeah," Grant said. "He shaved his head again."

Turco grinned and told Grant that the skinhead owed him forty bucks. He grabbed his board and charged into the cold water, slicing through the chop that pounded the inside. The water was warmer than he had anticipated; the waves lapping against his chest and face, refreshing in contrast to the chilly winds. It wasn't until reaching the dark swells that Turco spotted the shark's marble body. Its fin, worn. Cracked. Scarred by fishing lines and coral.

A boy on the jetty made the shark and called out to the others. Surfers began paddling back to shore.

Turco pulled a small piece of wax from the nose of his board, shaping it into a rock. He watched the animal's quick, darting movements, planning when to throw the wax.

He'd been attacked only once.

It was a baby thresher and he was twelve. The shark had taken a good chunk of flesh off his calf. Turco had to abandon his board and swim to the rock jetty before the shark could frenzy from blood. The rocks had torn him up and by the time he had arrived at the emergency room, two quarts of blood had drained from his body. His father's insurance could only cover part of the deductible. His father cursed Turco for having been attacked by the thing. He was in a hospital bed with blood staining the sheets and machines hummed and whined.

He'd lie silent in bed, trembling in pain medication and thought about the shark.

A month after his attack, he returned to the jetty and camped out on the beach for the better part of two days. He had taken his father's gun from the closet and stole a box of bullets from K-Mart. It was early morning, around five, the sun having barely made itself known when Turco spotted a small, baby dorsal flickering around in the shallows. He kept aim for some time before pulling the trigger and firing three rounds. Two shots caught its flesh and it stammered in the surf like a rabid dog before winding down, becoming motionless in the water. Gulls descended and fed.

It was the first thing he had ever killed.

He watched the shark now, carving through the water. As its narrow form circled by, Turco extended his arm, throwing the wax rock, hitting the shark's fin. The creature bucked and turned and altered its course, gravitating to deeper ocean.

The surfers who'd been spooked by the shark's sight quickly regrouped, falling into line behind Turco. Glancing up to the end of the pier, Turco spotted the three girls from earlier that morning they'd seen on the highway. The brunette grinned and waved to him. She was sipping a cherry Slurpie, leaning against the railing with her sunburned legs. Turco pointed to where the shark had been swimming and she nodded because she had seen Turco throw the piece of sex wax.

On the inside break, Grant paired with Marco Keyes. They sat up straight on their boards, watching the F-15s fire across sky. Rocket thunder came and went. The thunder was followed by a subdued ripple that echoed across the landscape and sent gulls crying.

Marco looked at Grant, who was shaking from a chilly breeze that had swept over the water. He told Grant he was going to freeze up sitting like that.

"I'm not too cold."

"Bullshit," Marco said. "Cold as witch's tit. Ugly ass witch to boot. Record temp put some fuckin frost on that shuttle."

Grant didn't answer, staring across to the outside break where Turco was sizing up an approaching set. From the distance, it looked like a large wall of green film.

Marco watched Turco paddle his way through the small line of locals. The wave was building force behind him and he began to race for it.

"Turco tells me it's your B Day. How old?"

"Nineteen."

Marco dug a nail into a piece of sex wax stuck on the tip of his board. "Time to party."

"Yep."

Marco grinned and ducked his head under water. "Shit. I can barely remember twenty-one. Once thirty hits, you're looking at this place a whole, helluva lot different."

"Time flies when you're having fun."

"The fuck it does."

Marco spit a wad of wax into the saltwater and a small wave passed and he went into formation. He changed his mind and let the wave pass beneath his board. "Shuttle totally fucked the patterns. Can't get an ounce of goddamn cutback on these chops. All that NASA shit in the water."

Grant told him how the turnpike had looked earlier that morning, bumper to bumper. People were fighting on the highway.

"Goddamn figures," Marco said. "One blow out and the world shakes." He shook his head. "Saw this coming a fuckin mile away."

They watched Turco finally break away from the top of the wave and drop down its face.

Marco splashed water onto his sunburned back. He motioned to Turco who was carving the face of the wave. "Boy's lookin good. Gonna make finals, right?"

Grant nodded. "Looks that way."

Marco studied the sky. From the distance, the miniscule black spots of F-15s turned on a dime, banking for another run. "You'd think they'd postpone it after this bullshit."

Grant didn't answer. He glanced up at a lone recovery chopper that flew across the skyline. He could make out a man dressed in military fatigues, clinging to the side with grappling lines and he was barking into a big walkie-talkie and pointing to something north of the pier.

Another wave rose on the outside, churning and tumbling into a wall of water. It was everywhere, stronger than any wave they'd seen that day.

Marco hollered. He slapped Grant's back and paddled into formation. "Got some good swells out'a it, right?"

Before Grant could say they had, Marco caught the edge of the wave and disappeared into the drop.

Perched alone, far from his brother and two cousins, Morgan Newnight had been in the water for the better part of two hours. In was on the outside break, just off the pier's endpoint that he spotted the thin line of swell that had rapidly transformed into a moving, building wall of glassy water. He watched the wave's crest grow and ascend. He could feel the current working its way right and he hadn't anticipated the face would be so strong and smooth for a low-basin jetty section.

The tide channel was situated at the base of Canaveral Sound and its opposing currents, dense and fast, gave way to exotic swells that could hold their strength for hours after the winds had blown the morning sessions out. He had read that only Tahiti and an island off the coast of Africa had had the same influence.

Firing down the white foam, Morgan began his foot plant. His tendency was to ride left. He hadn't anticipated the sudden shift in weight when the fucker in blonde dreadlocks dropped in. The impact was slight and immediate, strong enough to send Morgan spiraling over, plunging into the cold surge and he was thrown far down onto the ocean floor. He struck his head on small chunks of coral and the sting was immediate and water charged into his lungs and for a moment, he had forgotten how to swim.

Lost beneath the surface, tumbling in the water's power, Morgan could only cover his bleeding head and wait out the long, airless seconds. He felt as though he'd been buried far beneath the earth. Another jagged slice to his back. Coral tore into his flesh and he fought his way through the white foam, struggling for the surface. He kept his eyes closed; His lungs, strained and heavy, ready to explode. The lacerations in his head and back felt as long as string and burned. Digging, crawling through the currents, he could no longer hold his breath. Saltwater poured into his lungs as he broke to surface and the crisp, winter air clung to him. Coughing, gasping through the quick chop, he caught the fleeting image of Brian Turcorelli slicing apart the hump of wave.

On the beach, wrestling out from the shallow currents, Turco threw his board to the sand. He fumbled for the zipper on the back of his wetsuit. A bright, red strip of rash from a jellyfish was beginning to show itself upon his leg and he quickly put wet sand on the burn. Back in the water, he had caught a glimpse of the jellyfish clinging to the bottom of the wave as it rolled into formation. The wave was the biggest he had caught that month and he wondered how many people had seen it break. He knew there were photographers on the pier and that they'd probably taken some good shots of his cutbacks.

Through the bleak sunlight, he spotted one of the three girls hanging on the pier railing. She was the smallest of the three. Blond, pretty, plump as a mushroom. She wore a feathered roach clip in her hair that she'd bought on the pier.

When Turco waved to her, she burst out into a giggle. She motioned the brunette over, who was picking through some postcards on a rack just outside the pier giftshop.

Turco threw his wetsuit to the sand. He grunted and the girl laughed. The brunette and the taller blond came to their friend's side and all three were now watching Turco.

One of them shouted that he was supposed to have met them at the pier.

"Was I?"

"Doobie, remember?"

The brunette leaned over the pier railing. Her shoulders were deeply sunburned. She had finished her Slurpie and was using it for an ashtray and she asked Turco where his friend was.

"Which one?"

"You know which one!"

Before he could answer, a voice suddenly rose from behind his back: "Hey."

Morgan Newnight threw his board to the sand. He was shaking; his eyes wide and red. A red strip of blood hung over his left brow and his back wore jagged, bloody patterns of coral. He pointed a finger into Turco's eyeline. "That was pretty fuckin uncool."

Turco glanced around. Flies swarmed across his face and he struck them away. He faced Morgan. "I know you, bro?"

"Yeah, you know me." Blood ran from a cut on his lip. "Cut me off, asshole."

"Who you calling an asshole?"

"You, dick." Morgan took a step closer. Afternoon sunlight filled his face exposing a small scar that crept down the left side of his cheek. "Dickhead."

"Now I'm a dickhead."

"That's right."

"The dickhead asshole that cut you off."

"Dude, fuck you." Morgan spit blood into the sand. "I should kick your ass."

Crowds formed and beachcombers had stopped collecting shells and were now watching. A long wind rushed over the beach, sending spirals of sand across the flats. The sun slipped into clouds and it was suddenly cold.

Turco squinted from the sand and looked back at Morgan. He put out his hands. "All right, man. I didn't see you, okay?"

"You seeing me now?"

"Dude, calm down-"

"Dude, fuck you, are you fucking seeing me now?" He motioned to the blood running down his forehead.

Turco swallowed a breath, picking salt from his lower lip. "Look, I know you can kick my ass. I don't want to fight."

"Then why'd you do that shit out there?"

"I don't wanna fight."

"I'll fuckin ask again. Why'd you-"

Turco cracked Morgan in the face. It was a head butt and blood bubbled out through Morgan's nostrils and ran down his face.

Turco struck again, kicking Morgan high in the stomach. They both doubled over and fell to the wet sand.

Blinded by blood, Morgan shielded himself. The blows were quick, frantic. Before he could rise, Turco kicked him in the face.

The sand was rough, pulverized pebbles, staining Morgan's bloody jaw. He covered his nose, frantic to contain the blood from spilling out. It was running everywhere and small children backed away, never having seen blood so red and fresh. Someone screamed out Turco's name and he kicked Morgan in the mouth and teeth sliced his toe and he fell to his knees. He threw Morgan's face into dried remains of Man O' War. The poison was strong. Boils, red and bulging, began to form on his face and neck. He screamed and Turco spit on him.

"Wanna fuck with me?!"

He threw quick punches into the back of Morgan's head.

On the pier, the girls watched, stunned. Locals jumped to the sand to get a closer look and some tourists had stopped taking photos of the shuttle cloud.

Voices sounded off around Turco and he couldn't hear them. The ocean and dunes. The pier and parking lot. Things quieted. The wind rushed over his body, shielding him. He screamed and his fists, red with blood, pummeled like cannery machines.

Morgan became dazed, unable to cover his face from the blood and poison. His skin fell numb, grotesquely swollen. Bruises shined in the afternoon sunlight. The world was silent and he could feel wind and the warm blood.

Turco screamed: "Goddamn squid! This ain't your tribe!"

Locals hollered and cussed and children found the backs of beach umbrellas to hide in. A boy darted by Turco, shouting his name and he ran into the foaming beach water.

Turco stumbled up, kicking Morgan in the stomach. "This ain't your tribe, cocksucker!" He threw Morgan's board into the parking lot, tearing off the nose. Bystanders began to key the sides of cars and a teenage girl in tie-dye jumped up on the hood of a rusted Dodge pick-up.

Locals smashed bottles across the parking lot and busted windows of the pier gift shop.

Helicopters broke across the sky and one of the pilots spotted the commotion and called it in. The crowds slipped away before two officers from the Shore Patrol arrived in ATVs.

By the time his brother and two cousins had found him hiding in the dunes, Morgan had finished throwing up the blood he'd swallowed.

❦❦❦

They took the three girls to Murphy's Saddle Pub off Ocean and A1A. Grant had worked dry-wall the summer before and was friendly with the daytime bartender.

The bartender was a transplant from North Carolina.

He had come to Nation Beach three years ago and met a local girl, a waitress at the pub. They moved in together and it was months later that she had become pregnant. She had gotten him a job and they'd begun talking about ways to save money for the baby. A week later, a drunk from Titusville had struck her on the side of A1A. The bartender had spent the remainder of his savings on her funeral because her mother had passed away and there was no money. He moved into a one-unit down the street, a block from the pier. Besides the bar, he had found a job working part-time dry wall and had met Grant. He kept a small photo of the girl next to the register.

The bartender had brought them a new pitcher and gave it to Grant.

Harlan sat with the brunette whose fake ID gave the name Lynn Fowler.

Harlan told her it was a bad fake and he laughed and rubbed his face because it had become warm from the beer. He asked her if the ID had worked in Palm Beach.

"All the time," she answered.

Grant sat beside her two friends. Both wore their hair in Jamaican braids and the shortest called herself Chloe. Grant knew the name was a put-on and she drank beer, giggling and humming something from The Smiths and she'd shout out names to some of the songs that played on the juke box and clung to Grant's side.

Harlan brought another pitcher of Coors back from the bar and Chloe watched the beer pour into her cup and she asked Harlan what else there was to do in Nation Beach.

"Drink and get stoned."

She nodded and closed her eyes because she was spinning from the beer. She stared at the sailfish hanging above the bar and grinned. She said: "I can see that."

Grant lit another cigarette, staring at the taller blond. Her face was half-obscured under her cinnamon-blonde strands of hair and acne hid under a deep tan. They had been trading glances at one another.

Grant pulled a cigarette for her and she took it. She hadn't touched her beer.

"You drinking?" Harlan asked.

"No, thanks." She lit her cigarette from Grant's.

Harlan looked at her full cup. Layers of spent foam slid down its side and he thought of melting snow and he began to laugh. "It's beer."

"I can see that."

"You're not paying for it."

"I know." She took a drag of the cigarette. "I just don't feel like drinking, okay?"

Harlan wiped peanut shells off the table. He used his shirt to clean up the mess from his beer. He turned to Grant. "Free beer, I don't get it."

"She doesn't want to drink," Grant said; his voice hoarse and tongue thick. When he pushed his own beer aside, Harlan shook his head and mumbled.

The tall blond looked away and the juke box pulled up a song from Pink Floyd and Chloe began to sway to it.

Harlan gulped down the last of his beer. He tucked brown curls of hair into the tops of his ears and poured a new beer for the brunette. "Here ya're, Lynn."

The brunette drew a deep breath. She was sick and she struggled against the nausea. She told him that her name wasn't really Lynn.

Harlan went to fill her friend's cup.

"No! I don't want any!"

Lynn snapped: "What is your problem, Megan?"

She fell quiet. There was fear in her eyes and she tried not to look up from the table. She killed the cigarette in a plastic ashtray that was shaped like an alligator, gesturing to Turco, who was standing at a pay phone across the bar. "Your friend," she said. "He's a psycho. Whaled all over that guy."

At the pay phone, Turco let the cigarette burn between his fingers. He listened to the voice on the other end of the phone and the words were chopped, strung together. He pressed the phone receiver to his ear and the voice began to shout at him and Turco had to put the phone receiver down and let it pass. When the voice fell quiet, Turco asked where he was.

The voice went on. Turco waited for the next opportunity to speak. When it came, he said: "Yeah, Rick, I know he's pissed. The shit's all over the street. Why- why is he so-"

The voice wouldn't let him finish. It asked Turco another question.

"No, yeah," Turco answered. "I got the money but I gotta give it to him Monday." He shook his head. "No, Monday."

He checked his Timex.

"It's like, three-thirty."

The voice went on.

Turco spat on the floor, kicking a Styrofoam cup. He kept the phone receiver to his ear and waited for his turn to speak. Wrinkled posters of space shuttles and surfers hung on the wood-paneled walls and he occasionally glanced at them. He threw the cigarette to the bar's floor. "Look Rick, I know he's pissed. That's why I need to talk with him, okay?"

Grant walked past the bar, past the juke box, setting an empty pitcher on the counter. He moved up to the pay phone, watching Turco's face go cold. There was a stiffness in his breath, heavy and dry. Grant thought he might have been choking.

Turco turned into the wall and listened to the voice. Grant could hear the word Overtown.

"Overtown?" Turco whispered. "Why'd he go to-"

The voice told him to quiet down. It went on about a reggae concert and Haitians. It mentioned a name.

Turco repeated the name: "Temba."

Grant lit a cigarette. He gestured something to Turco. Turco put a hand up to quiet him. He pulled bangs from his face and his hair was dry and bleached from the salt water, looking like the tangled hair of a toddler.

The voice cussed and told him to call him later; after six, on his beeper.

Turco nodded. "Yeah, all right." He rubbed fingers over his nose and mouth. "I'll make sure he gets it tonight." He hung up only after the line had gone dead.

Grant took a cigarette from Turco's pack. He looked to the floor, striking the match. "What's up?"

Turco scratched his chin stubble, staring at the pay phone. "Rick says Vay's working for Temba."

"Temba Mills?"

Turco nodded. "In Overtown."

Grant paused. He had heard about Temba from Vay. Temba was behind some of the things from Lockhart Beach and Davie Speedway and he often suspected Turco was selling his weed but had never asked about it.

Grant took a drag of his cigarette and asked Turco about the money from the ATM.

"It's all gone to shit." Turco grabbed his cigarettes from off the pay phone. He whispered something that Grant couldn't make out and walked off.

"Vay never told you?" Harlan asked.

Turco shook his head. "Didn't tell me shit." He positioned the cue ball at the rear of the pool table. He checked his angles and chalked his stick. "Like I'm supposed to know I was selling some Haitian-monkey's skunk weed. Whole thing's a pigshit circus."

He struck white ball and it was a bad split down the center.

A busload of German tourists had wandered in from Kelly's Lobster Trap across the street. They wore red tee shirts that advertised a BBQ restaurant in Huntington Beach and on the backs of their tee shirts, a cartoon pig was roasting a chicken on a spitfire grill. The German tourists asked questions to the bartender about the space shuttle.

Turco called stripes and began to clear the pool table. He cracked a ball into the side pocket, loud enough to warrant glances from the Germans. The girls were at the juke box and AC/DC filled the bar.

Grant put new quarters into the table and he racked again.

Turco slammed the break and balls tore across the felt and the sound boomed across the table.

Harlan stood in silence, watching the balls find pockets. He took another sip of beer before asking Turco if Temba was behind the thing in Davie.

Turco didn't answer, calling his shot and sending the three balls off the rail and into the left side pocket.

Harlan asked again about Temba.

"Don't worry about it." Turco shot two more balls before missing the twelve.

AC/DC screamed.

The girls had put another dollar into the machine and were going through new selections. Chloe began shouting the lyrics to a Crowded House song.

"Lynn's got a thing for me," Harlan said.

"Guess she likes the junior-college material."

Harlan grinned but it was awkward and he soon became silent and moved away from the pool table and began taking small sips of his beer.

Grant saw this and told Turco to fuck off. "Harlan's gonna write Moby Dick. He's got talent, he's gonna make some money."

Harlan looked away. One of the girls had heard this and asked Harlan about his writing.

"Guy writes poems," Grant said.

Turco told Grant to shut up.

"You ever read his poems?"

Turco shrugged and prepared his next shot.

"The guy writes some amazing shit," Grant said. "Gonna make some money."

Turco lined up the cue ball, slamming the twelve into the pocket. He nodded. He said: "I'm gonna make some money, too." He glanced at the neon Budweiser clock on the wall. "Make some tonight."

The Germans laughed at the bartender's joke about Ronald Reagan and a woman asked about the girl in the photograph.

They took a group photo under the sailfish above the bar.

4:01 P.M.

It was 1864 and forward camps of the Confederacy, led by Colonel Roland Pierce, laid claim to the shores east of Orlando and designated many of the Seminole territories as army fortitudes. A small, disorganized protest by the local tribes had led to an uprising. Pierce ordered the execution of the tribe's Chieftain. The Seminole tribes countered with a night attack that killed 40 soldiers. The following morning, Confederates organized a surprise assault on the neighboring tribes, killing any Seminole that still wore warrior colors. By sunset, the army had burned the mutilated refuse, interring the surviving tribes people to labor camps in the sawgrass areas. Their eldest sons would be indentured and fight for the cause. There was a plaque that told the story of the Pierce-Seminole massacre, built on a sand dune that rose above the boardwalk leading to its beaches. It had since been removed, replaced with a restroom shack. A nature trail wound into the marsh and ended at the beach parking lot.

Point Dune was the name of the place where Seminoles were slaughtered and the name had since been changed to Red Dunes Park to pacify the condo developers.

Chloe and Turco spent another ten minutes in the bar's parking lot smoking cigarettes. They talked about a Social D concert in Miami and Turco got a blowjob and Chloe had told him not to tell her friends and Turco said he didn't care either way.

By the time they'd met up with the others at the Red Dunes' picnic area, Chloe was sick from the beer and Lynn took her to the public restroom where she vomited. There was no toilet paper and the faucet was broken and Lynn took her to a water fountain to clean her face.

When Chloe returned to the picnic area, she made a point of ignoring Turco. "How do I get a piece of the shuttle?" she asked Harlan.

"Go for a swim."

Megan laughed.

"No," Chloe said. She stared at one of the picnic grills. "I'm serious. We came up here to get a piece of the shuttle... shuttle thing."

"I came here to ditch English 3," Lynn said. She popped a piece of gum, twisting it over in her teeth.

Turco checked his watch and gestured at Grant. He told Grant they had to go.

Harlan stumbled off one of the picnic tables and tripped over a piece of bark and Lynn laughed. Harlan flashed Turco the joint in his pocket. "Just rolled this."

"Hey, man, we gotta go!" Turco threw on his tanktop and pulled his cigarettes and Chloe stared at him.

When Turco said it again, she shouted: "Chill out! It's not like you have some place to be!"

Turco lit a cigarette and faced Chloe with eyes that fell through her. He turned to the distant NASA launch towers hanging on the north. They were bathed in a gray mist, no longer distinguishable among the departure grids. They were antennas, rising up into a matte-blue sky that had since darkened. He turned back to Chloe. "What do you mean by that?"

Chloe didn't answer. She crossed her arms against the strong gusts of ocean wind. She realized a small spot of vomit was visible on her knit top and she quickly wiped it clean.

Turco stepped towards Chloe. He was grinning dangerously and his arms were extended out to her as though they were going to embrace. "We have no place to be. What does that mean?"

"Forget it."

"No. What'd you mean by that?"

"I didn't mean anything."

"No. It's okay. You said we had no place to be." He faced Grant who was sitting on a table beside Megan. "That's what she said. Right, Grant?"

"Turco, it's nothing."

Turco put out a hand. "No. According to Chloe, we have no place to be."

Chloe's face flushed. She backed away, frightened.

Lynn smiled. "What she means is we're getting stoned and chilling out."

Turco kept his eyes on Chloe and she was crying.

"You think we're a bunch'a hicks?" Turco said. "Waiting for the next Burger King to open up down the block?"

Chloe dry-heaved and she was no longer able to vomit and she began searching for the shuttle trail but it was obscured in clouds.

"Waiting for a shitty Burger King?" Turco said.

"That's not what she meant!" Megan said.

"Shut up, bitch." He pointed to her. "Go back to your fucking Cabriolet and your SATs and West Palm." He snatched the joint from Harlan's fingers. He trudged past the sand dunes and vanished down a pathway.

❦❦❦

Lucas Turcorelli was born with an oxygen deficiency and to supplement this, the body pumped additional blood into the skull that caused unpredictable reactions to the nervous system. After four operations, doctors drilled holes into the skull to release blood resin and the deficiency had equalized. There would be permanent retardation, but he would retain some motor skills. A feeding tube was inserted into his body and a respirator would breathe for him.

Mary Turcorelli had found a night job packaging mail orders at a tee shirt shop in the Dry Hills Mall. On weekends, she'd stay additional hours, prepping the Monday-morning sendoffs, leaving Lucas to the custody of his older brother. A nurse from the insurance provider had helped Turco orient himself with the various duties. These consisted mainly of cleaning and changing things, monitoring the respirator that was attached to Lucas' wheelchair and seeing that his brother was being properly nourished. The feeding proved the most difficult. The food was a formula that required a skill in mixing powders and liquids and if the mixture wasn't correctly applied, the body would reject it and a seizure would result. One difficult summer had seen four seizures and Mary Turcorelli contemplated putting Lucas into private care. Turco convinced her to keep his brother home. He'd learn to mix the chemicals. He'd learn to work the tubes and feed Lucas intravenously.

The products were expensive to maintain and Turco shoplifted the powders and nutrients. He was caught one morning in the Cocoa Wallgreen's and arrested and it was his first official charge. When he turned sixteen, he started making money selling dope and on weekends, he'd put the money in his mother's drawer.

By seventeen, he was making good money.

Mary was able to quit her night job. She had again posed the question of putting Lucas into private care and again, Turco shot it down. As long as the insurance held out, they'd be able to manage the deductible.

Lucas could stay with him and every Saturday Turco could take him to the dock and show him the surf.

❦❦❦

Standing alone at the end of the jetty, Turco watched choppers roar above the shore in pairs. He had smoked the last of the joint. He thought about his brother and how he'd laugh from the roar of the choppers. He didn't hear Grant approach from behind. He turned into him and Grant asked if everything was okay.

Turco kept silent and when Grant asked again, Turco shrugged and let a moment pass and stared into the water. He moved closer to Grant, burying his hands in his surf trunks.

"I have to get that money to Vay," Turco said. "Something might happen if I don't get him his money. That H.A. owed Temba a lousy three pounds'a skunk." He kicked a pebble off the jetty rock, into the water. He squinted from the wind and sun. "I need that money, you know?"

Grant nodded. "I know."

Turco inhaled a deep breath of ocean air. He stared out to Monster Hole's dying outside. The packs of surfers had drifted far north and gulls swooped and dove for the dead remains of Man O War.

Turco studied his hand. It was dry and bits of skin were beginning to peel white. Fresh cuts gave way on his knuckles from the fight with the Seminole and he touched a stinging piece of open flesh, picking small bits of sand from the cut. He began to remember the dream and he took a deep breath and spat into the water. He told Grant about the dream. "It was this place. Black and red, like." He wiped his face clean of sweat and he looked at Grant. "It was like hell or something. I could feel it," he said. "It felt like hell. It was dark. I couldn't breathe."

Grant listened. He stared at Turco's fist.

"It's hard." Turco rubbed his dirty knuckles. "I feel like everyone's watching me and it's hard to breathe." He shook his head. The pot was heavy, disgusting to the taste and the back of his neck itched from sun and saltwater.

"Christ." Turco stared off to the road, barely visible in the folds of seagrape trees. "I wish I had a car. Get me out from all this shit."

Grant said nothing. He studied the choppers. In the distance, the shuttle's vapor trail of rocket smoke clung to the horizon.

Grant turned back to Turco. He asked Turco what he had meant about getting some money.

"Nothing. Don't worry about it."

"What?"

"It's your birthday, don't worry about it."

"Tell me."

Turco looked at him. He let a moment pass, then he pulled a crumpled pack of cigarettes from the back of his surf trunks. He winced from a new strip of sunburn. He said Save It All.

It was a convenience store, two blocks from the pier. A familiar place; they had skated there as boys. Libby's father had once delivered beer to the store when he had worked for the packaging company. The back lot was full of broken-down boxes and cement pilings and they'd go through the dumpster to find stale packs of cigarettes. Friday nights, they'd wait for strangers to come along and buy them 12-packs.

It was 10:25 when Turco had entered the store. He was getting a Gatorade at the cooler when he saw the store manager winding the day's receipt tape at the register. It was close to 10:30 when he spied the manager heading into the back room with a metal box stuffed under his arm. The box was small enough, easy to carry with a tin handle and that was the first thing Turco had noticed.

He moved behind the Icee machine with his skateboard dangling from his fingers. He was good at hiding, disappearing into things; pretending to read magazines, glancing from time to time at the closed door where he was sure the safe was kept. When the manager returned from the back, he'd have a new drawer of cash and he gave that drawer to the night guy behind the register and left in his Cressida.

Turco made a habit to time it every night he returned. 10:30, except for Sundays. Same routine: metal box, back room, new drawer.

Metal box, back room, new drawer.

He'd hum it skating home, or paddling into water. It was something consistent. He visualized the metal box with the tin handle.

Metal box, back room, new drawer.

"The guy's back there for close to five minutes," Turco said. "Then he returns with a new drawer. I came back there the next night after skating with Fleet. Sure enough, the dude came back. Same thing. Metal box, back room, new drawer."

"Metal box, back room, new drawer," Grant said.

"Four nights I watched this." Turco held up his fingers. "Every night at 10:25, right on time."

"That doesn't mean shit."

"No, you're wrong. There's a safe back there. Time-release shit. Company must have it set for 10:30."

"You're guessing."

"The hell I am. The old man brings reserve cash to the store for the night shift, locks it in the safe. All we gotta do is be there when it happens."

"You're serious about this."

"Why the fuck wouldn't I be?"

"Because it's too much of a risk."

"It's simple, Grant."

"No, it's a hassle." Grant moved away. He stared into the water, made rough from the afternoon winds. He looked back at Turco. "It's extreme."

"Not if there's three of us."

Grant paused. He studied Turco; the small cuts from the fight with the Seminole. His hair had become bleached from the sun and salt air and he could smell the pot on his breath.

"Get this," Turco said. "We have one guy ready in the car, in the parking lot with the engine running. We got a guy keeping a gun on the dick behind the counter. Making sure that bitch is away from the alarm button under the register." He slapped Grant's shoulder. "The last guy's in the back with the manager. Has him open the metal box, safe, everything. All the shit goes in two bags."

"Two bags."

"Yeah."

"You've already decided on two bags."

"Yeah, I did."

Grant thought about it. The distance to the counter. The size of the safe box. The exit doors.

He could see the store around him. Candy aisle with the unopened Snickers boxes. Icee machine and tracks of magazines. The florescent lights shining down. The distance of the beer coolers to the door and the mirrors in the corners.

The entire store and everyone in it flashed through his brain and he began to understand.

Turco made a gun gesture. "When all the shit's in the bags, everyone goes to the ground. We give 'em the order to count to fifty, a hundred. Some shit like that." He nodded as to convince himself. "And they'll do it."

Grant looked off to a gull making circles over the dunes. The bird cried into the open sky, ducking down upon a piece of seaweed.

"Five minutes later," Turco said, "the car's heading south on A1A, mission accomplished." He pulled a cigarette from his ear and put it to his lips. "Three-man job with a car. We'll get Reece to drive. He needs a nut after getting fucked-over on that construction job with the Holiday Inn. So do you."

Grant fell quiet, watching the horizon. The shuttle smoke was beginning to evaporate, the wind growing stagnant.

Turco cleared his throat. He let a moment pass before asking the question. "Have you and Libby even talked about money?"

Grant snapped to him.

Turco lit the cigarette. He was shaking from the chill and he told Grant that abortions cost money.

"Shut your mouth," Grant said, loud enough to spook the gulls.

"Brother, I'm your friend," Turco said. "I'm just saying-"

"Libby and me ain't your business, Turco. You got that?"

Turco said nothing and looked away.

Grant spat into the wind and cussed. He kicked a rock into the water.

Turco offered him a cigarette and Grant refused it.

"Whether or not you keep the kid," Turco said, "you'll need money."

"You don't talk about these things to me," Grant said. "You don't bring this up again."

Turco killed his cigarette. He told Grant he wouldn't bring it up.

A patrol helicopter, rotors whumping, shot through the sky. Grant said something that was lost in the craft's noise. He walked off, leaving Turco to stand alone against the ocean.

5:31 P.M.

The sting had left him and he no longer paid attention to the pain.

His nose was badly bruised, not broken. He had been in worse fights. His brother was a good fighter. His father was also a man who hit hard. He remembered as a child, killing the crow in the parking lot where Bruce Bearwolf sold fireworks. He hadn't meant to strike the bird with the rock. He never imagined his throw would have the impact. It was dumb luck. He had stood still and watched it flutter on the ground, its wings clutching for air. He had heard its caw, fast and erratic like a machine winding down.

His father, sitting in the pick-up, saw it fall to the ground. He didn't run from his father. It was something he had learned never to do.

The man beat him in front of the fireworks stand and the tourists pretended not to see it and the man stuffed the dead crow in his face. He cursed him for killing the thing.

Later, locked in the small tool shed behind the trailer, he sat in silence. He felt proud for having killed the crow, how perfectly the rock had struck the bird. How it had spun, dropped to the ground.

He sat in the shed for hours. His eyes never adjusted to the darkness and the heat stung and he pictured the crow, dead on the pavement. Black eyes. Wings arched. A red ink blot of sticky blood and gnats. It put him to sleep.

His two cousins, Jessie and Mark, sat on dunes and threw rocks into the thin sand stream that flowed into the ocean.

Morgan could hear the chip of the rocks skipping on the ocean's flat surface. He sat on the hood of his '78 Firebird, tee-shirt pressed against his swollen nose. The blood had stopped flowing. The pressure had given him a bad sinus headache and his face felt like dough. He couldn't feel his lower lip. There was some blood and it was dried into cake.

His brother Will finished racking the boards into the pick-up truck. Tattoos wound across his neck and chest, ending at the waist where his wetsuit hung. He fished a cigarette out of the truck's dashboard and he looked at Morgan and smirked.

"You gonna sit there all day like a beat-up squid? What's this fucker even look like?"

Morgan said nothing. He pressed the shirt harder into his nose and coughed. Mucus was building up in his chest.

Will moved into his little brother's shadow. He pulled the tee shirt from Morgan's face, exposing his badly swollen nose and mouth.

"Look at this shit," Will said.

Jessie and Mark glanced at them from the dune. From the distance, they appeared as twig figures and they continued throwing rocks into the beach.

"Look what that local redneck did to you." Will grabbed Morgan by the throat, pulling him around to face his reflection in the Firebird's tint. "You gonna just let this lie?"

"I don't know who he is!" Morgan barked. He wiped the dried blood from his lip and his nose was a bruised purple.

"We gonna find out."

"No one's talking."

"Little brother, you're gonna find out who this bitch is."

"This isn't our beach," Morgan said. "I don't know no one here."

Will paused. He had a strong urge to strike his brother across the face. He let go of Morgan's neck, lighting his cigarette, look over the sand dunes.

"You should'a shouted," Eric said. "I would'a heard you from the truck."

"I didn't need your help," Morgan mumbled.

"The hell you didn't." He threw a match to the dirt.

Morgan wiped his eyes. He stared at his bare feet.

The afternoon shadows had lengthened across the dunes and Will shook his head and spat tobacco to the dirt. He told Morgan to clean up and go home.

Morgan stood silent; his skin, sun-burned, blistered. Man-O-War poison was everywhere on his skin and it stung and burned in the sun.

A gull rushed by overhead and he ducked and his cousins laughed under their breath.

Morgan moved up to Will and told him that their father would have been proud.

"The hell you talking about, Morgan?"

"I defended this beach. This shit belongs to us." He got into Will's face. "You remember all those maps and shit he had?" He pointed far into the distance, past the beach pathway leading out onto A1A. "All them reservation points as far south as Kendall?"

Will took a drag of his cigarette. He glanced at Jessie and Mark and they were moving around Morgan's Firebird.

"He said it was gonna come back to us," Morgan said. "Return. Fuckin believed it."

"That was liquor talking," Will said. "Old man couldn't even make the payments on that horse trailer and he thought all this was ours. Selling fireworks on A1A. That was where all that shit ended. You gotta get that through your head."

Morgan stared out to the beach. "I ain't gonna let them take it from us." He faced his brother. "You understand what I'm saying, Will?"

Jessie and Mark approached Will's pick-up truck. Jessie pulled a joint from the glove compartment. "Where we smoking this?"

"Morgan ain't smoking shit," Will said. "Look at his mouth."

Mark grinned. He kicked sand pebbles and dust onto Morgan's legs. "Does his pussy hurt, too?"

Morgan let a moment pass. He then threw his shirt and towel to the ground, pushing Will aside and climbed into his Firebird.

Mark laughed. "Did I offend you, little cousin?"

Morgan pulled the keys from the visor and charged the ignition. Exhaust fumes blew out of the muffler and Jessie cussed. He punched the trunk of the car.

Will clutched the open window panel and it was cool to the touch and he told Morgan to hold up.

"Get fucked, all of you."

Morgan fired the car into reverse and peeled out.

His brother held onto the window. "Morgan! Morgan, goddamn it!"

Morgan threw the Firebird into drive. He punched the gas and burned out onto the wet beach pavement of A1A.

❦❦❦

The lines had grown long and two of the registers had broken down.

The part-time help Libby hoped would arrive never came. Her manager had a temporary security guard working the door and much of their stock had been lost. They were able to recover the larger items; frozen meats and non-perishables. A wino from the Big Daddy's had tried to make off with a roll of lottery tickets and there was an off-duty cop in one of the checkouts and he arrested the man before he could disappear through the doors and children watched the arrest, curious and on guard.

Libby had been relegated to the far-off express checkout. The customers were sweating and complained about wasting time and had other things to do.

A woman in a Denny's uniform shoveled groceries out her cart and onto the checkout ramp. Her son, seven and red-faced, clung to the cart's side. He stared at Libby and Libby smiled back, running groceries over the laser scanner.

The woman in the Denny's uniform watched each item sweep through. The boy stared at the red laser.

"The Lucky Charms are marked down," the woman said.

"Yes, ma'am."

"Marked down a dollar."

"Yes, ma'am. That's what the machine's telling me."

The boy looked up at his mother. "Mommy."

The woman dug through her purse.

"Mommy."

"What?"

"They gonna send another shuttle up?"

The woman shook her head. "These Lucky Charms are costing me almost three dollars."

"Them people are dead?"

"Who?"

"The astronauts."

The woman looked at Libby. "What's the total?"

"Thirty-six twenty, ma'am."

"That's with the coupons?"

"Yes, ma'am."

"Jesus." The woman dug deeper through her purse.

"All them astronauts are dead," the boy said.

The echo of the supermarket's intercom fell over the crowded checkout aisles and Libby heard the swash of a mop from the ice machine.

The woman handed Libby two twenties and some change. Pennies fell to the floor and Libby scrambled to pick them up and the boy asked again about the astronauts.

Grant came through the doors, throwing a tee shirt over his head. He was sunburned and Libby could smell the ocean on him.

The woman shook her head. "Three dollars for them Lucky Charms, Greggy." She pulled her son off the shopping cart.

It moved within her and tickled. The sensation was just big enough that she couldn't ignore it and she'd smile. When they passed the aisle of baby care, she'd glance at the big, brick stacks of diapers. The tiny faces and bodies of the baby models seemed countless and she wondered how big such a thing could grow. Its first smile. She wanted to tell him these things, but she kept silent. Somewhere down the aisle, he had taken her hand in his.

Garbage and spilled food littered the linoleum floor. Beer cans, fat and pierced from the store's heat, overflowed in puddles. Grant stepped over them and opened a cooler and pulled out a 12-pack of Miller. He checked the ends for dents.

He asked her about the TV cameras.

"Channel Five. They're interviewing people who saw the shuttle go."

"Figures." He tucked the beer under his arm. "Wish they'd just leave it all alone." He crossed the aisle and began searching through bags of pretzels and potato chips. A large tin of popcorn had been broken and kernels were scattered across the aisle.

"You look tired," Libby said.

"Haven't slept."

"It's your birthday, Grant. You should call in sick tonight."

He shook his head and told her it was too late to call in. "Jess covered me last week. I gotta work his twelve-to-eight." He breathed hard, tearing through the remaining bags of pretzels. "Goddamn."

Libby found a bag in the back and pulled it out. Smaller bags fell to the floor and Grant went to pick them up.

"The roads are all blocked-up till tomorrow," Libby said. "Ain't gonna be busy at all. They won't miss you."

Grant checked the bag for any tears.

Libby moved closer, touching his arm. "Let's camp out tonight. At the beach."

"There's that party."

"You think that's still going on?"

Grant shrugged. "Far as I know."

"So you still wanna go to that."

"I don't know. Yeah, I guess. Why, don't you?"

"Not really."

"You feelin okay?"

She didn't answer.

"We don't have to go."

Libby shrugged. "We'll stay for a half hour, then leave."

Grant thought about it and said nothing. Lines of shoppers were on the checkouts and a portly man with faded-green army tattoos argued with Libby's manager. There was a moment when the man got dangerously close to the manager's face and a cashier called the security worker over and the man left.

"I might have to do some shit first," Grant said.

"Like what?"

Grant glanced at Libby's stomach. He could see that her hand was now cupping her waist and she smiled because she knew he was blushing. She said, "Nothing much to see yet." She moved closer, wrapping her hand around his arm. "But I think I felt it."

Another wave of announcements came across the store intercom and stockmen went off to collect spilled gallons of orange juice and milk.

"Is it still cold out there?" Libby asked.

Grant paused because he was thinking of the baby. "It's too early to feel anything," Grant said, putting a hand on Libby's stomach.

"I know, but- " She stammered and struggled. She withdrew her hand out from his arm and rubbed her eyes. "I feel something," she said.

Grant looked away for a moment. He said: "We talked about this."

"I know we did, I-"

"I thought we talked about all of this."

She started off.

"Libby."

Libby took another step and stopped. She began to sway.

Grant put the beer down and moved over to her. "What do you want? You have to tell me what you want."

She began to cry.

He went to hold her.

She moved away and wiped her eyes. A voice came on the intercom.

The hot air stunk of beer and the heat was eating through her polyester uniform.

"I can make it work," Grant said. "Either way, I can make it work."

"I don't know -- I'm scared." Her voice broke. "Those poor people. This day's made me scared."

An elderly woman moved by with a shopping cart and she saw Libby's red eyes and asked her if everything was all right and Libby nodded and the woman moved on.

"I'm scared," she told Grant again.

"I know." He went to hold her. He wiped tears from her face.

Libby faced him. She asked how much the abortion would cost.

"Maybe four hundred," he answered. He wasn't sure. He was frustrated and in the heat of the store it was hard to think about numbers.

Libby shook her head. "No, I mean -- if we keep it. How much for the hospital. If we keep it."

Grant wiped sweat from his hair. He breathed deeply and told her it was a lot.

Libby's uniform clung to her skin and her manager glared at her from the checkouts and taped his watch.

Libby nodded to him. "I gotta get back to work."

"Libby."

She kissed him and held his hand. "I wanted to give you your present," she said. "Now you gotta wait till tonight."

Grant nodded and he went to kiss her.

Libby moved away.

"C'mon," she said, "I'll ring you up."

The reporter wasn't one Turco recognized. He was tall, gaunt. A moustache nearly matched the color of his dusty hair. He held his microphone like a rolled up newspaper, putting it too close to his face. He talked quickly. The words sounded fake. Strung together. He asked Turco where he had been.

"At the pier." Turco felt the camera on him and it made him grin. "Blew up, like, right in front of me."

"A fireball," Harlan said. The camera panned to his face and made him twitch.

The reporter asked him to elaborate.

"It was sad to see," Harlan said.

"Yes." He gestured to Harlan to keep going.

"All that smoke in the air."

"How did you feel? When you saw it?"

"It's sad, you know?"

The man nodded. "Something you'll remember."

"Yeah." Harlan nodded. "Ripped apart, all over the sky." He wiped off a nervous grin. "Never saw nothing so-"

"Devastating?"

Harlan absorbed the word. He nodded. "It was very devastating."

They sat in the apartment living room, watching their faces fill the television.

Turco popped open his beer. He glanced at Harlan and said: "I think that faggot likes you." He motioned to the television. "Look how he keeps shoving that mic in your mouth. Wants you to suck it."

"Fuck off." Harlan sealed the joint and he shook his head when Turco called him a faggot.

The report cut to an image of the shuttle's vapor trail and the camera panned down onto the Winn-Dixie parking lot. Grant's face filled the screen and Turco laughed and spit beer. He wiped his chin and hollered. He shouted to Grant that he was on television.

"Check out Grant's face," Harlan said.

"Dude, he looks like a goddamn blowfish."

Harlan laughed. He watched Grant answer a question and he realized Grant was good at nodding.

Turco said: "Blowfish with dyed-black hair."

Grant came out of his bedroom, throwing on a tee shirt. There was a moment when he had fallen asleep and there was drowning and he couldn't move his body and he had screamed and the scream awoke him and he had heard Turco shouting.

He fetched a beer from the refrigerator. He moved over to where Turco and Harlan were sitting.

"Look," Turco said, pointing to the television. "They got Libby."

Grant stared into the television at Libby's face. Her hair was caught in the wind and she talked about a temporary power blackout at the supermarket and some elderly woman fainting. She was holding back tears and she cupped a hand over her stomach and her bangs fell into her face and she brushed them away.

"She looks good on TV," Turco said. "Lipstick shines through."

An elementary school principal spoke about children. There was a teacher and her students had written cards in crayons for her and some of the students knew that their teacher was killed and the principal began to cry.

"Fuck her," Turco said. "Those kids are loving life."

Harlan nodded. "No more homework for the rest of the year."

"No shit. Wish my teachers would'a blown up into oblivion-"

"Hey!" Grant kicked out a stool from the corner of the kitchen. It fell to the linoleum with a thud and Harlan snapped around and dropped the joint to the carpet.

Grant's face was white and glowing in the TV. He said, "That's a human life! That's a person nobody's gonna see again!"

"Grant, take it easy."

"Fuck you, Turk, show some respect."

"Fuck me? Dude fuck you."

"Why don't you think for a second before you open your fucking mouth."

"Grant-"

"Those people are dead. They're fucking dead!"

"Yeah, I know,I heard about that."

"Dead, asshole." Grant cursed and moved back into the kitchen and threw the rest of his beer into the sink.

Turco told him to come back into the living room.

Grant snatched up a bottle of Tylenol and a half-empty liter of Pepsi and returned to his bedroom.

It was on the 24th of January, four days shy of his sixteenth birthday when his mother died. It was in a hospital room in Cocoa Beach and it had been raining steady, four days straight. They had tried a final procedure to remove the growth. The cells had metastasized and found their way into the bone. The chemo and dehydration treatments had turned her body into a thin string of yarn and she had often joked about floating out of bed.

The days leading up to her passing were strange and difficult, sometimes filled with card games or visits from relatives he had met only once or twice in his life. There was a morning when the woman from the insurance company came and they talked about things Grant didn't want to hear about and then there were days he sat beside his mother and watched television while she slept.

He had seen her become overwrought with drugs.

He had been with her when she moaned and cried and burst out in harsh language. There were times when she'd vomit. The bile was green and he had to turn away and the nurse held her hand.

There were times when she felt well enough to take walks with him down hospital halls and she'd ask him what he had had for dinner, in the cafeteria. They'd stand at a large window at the end of the hall and stare out to the landfill that sat on a hill. The landfill was a mountain covered in grass swatches and it was beautiful and she said that they'd picnic there soon. They'd watch circles of crows and gulls feed on the trash and the garbage trucks sat in a long lines.

His mother would hold his hand.

She told him how she would miss their walks and he began to cry. He would walk her back to her hospital room and shut the television off so she could sleep.

Lying in his bed, Grant stared out the small apartment window. The top of the landfill rose above a billboard sign and a newer landfill had been built in Clinton Beach and most of the trucks had become rerouted. The grass had since been removed and now wore a rusty tinge and a single crane sat on its top. The crows had long disappeared and staring out to it, Grant realized the entire hill gave the impression of a pitcher's mound. Brown clay, deteriorating.

He swallowed three Tylenol tablets. He washed them down with warm Pepsi and lit a cigarette.

There was a knock at his door. Harlan moved carefully in and waved to Grant and asked him if he was okay.

Grant nodded that he was and felt his head. "Bullshit migraine. Tired as all hell."

Harlan moved closer. He put his hands in his jeans pockets. "Maybe you should get some sleep."

"Can't. Wired on overtime. Might as well wait the shit out."

Harlan nodded and through the apartment window, he could see Federal Highway and construction crews barricading the utility roads.

Grant saw Harlan's notebook and asked how the poem was coming along.

"Having some trouble. I think I smoked too much Turco weed."

Grant grinned and Harlan laughed. He told Grant it was hard to get things on paper. "Maybe it's not that good."

"That teacher you talked about. She said you have talent."

"I dunno. All teachers say that shit."

"I bet she's right."

Harlan looked nervous and turned back to the window. He scratched his face and he told Grant he'd keep working on the poem.

"I want to read it once it's done," Grant said. "You gonna have it done by tonight?"

"Yeah, I think so."

"What's it about?"

"Nothing," Harlan answered. He looked back out the window and changed his mind. "It's about the ocean. I think."

Grant and Turco stood on the breezeway, staring down into the apartment lot. Crows swooped down on the row of trash bins and Grant studied the one closest to the debris. It picked away at a bag of Oreos and others had managed to rip open a cardboard produce box.

Grant fumbled for a cigarette. "How much do you think they have?"

Turco wiped tobacco from his lips. For a moment, he wasn't sure. "At least two grand," he finally said. "There's also a few cashier's checks. Probably puts the daily count at three. With the combined week's nut, we're looking at ten grand."

Grant thought about the money. It'd be enough to cover expenses. It could buy Libby a room in the hospital and tests and the rest of the costs he'd cover himself. He'd saved up almost five hundred. A month more of double shifts and some dry wall could get him to a good place.

He lit a cigarette, sheltering the flame.

Turco helped cup the match. He said: "This isn't your problem, Grant. It's just a thing. I wanted you to know about it, that's all."

Grant watched the crows break from the trash bins. A car passed and a couple could be heard fighting in one of the apartments around the corner.

Turco drew a breath and rubbed his hands. He lit his cigarette off Grant's. He was sorry for what he said back on the jetty. "I didn't mean nothin'. This day, it's strange, you know?"

"Yeah."

"That shit I said about the teacher. I didn't mean that shit. I feel bad all of this happened in our backyard, you know? I don't know what to say about it, so I just say shit."

Grant nodded because he understood.

"You and Libby, you'll think of something. You're smart. You'll think of something."

Grant took a drag of the cigarette and pressed his fingers into his eyes. The headache was a cold, shooting block of pain. He regretted having had the beer and he closed his eyes and there was Libby standing at the checkout counter.

He told Turco he'd do it. "But you gotta get Reece to drive."

"Grant, you don't have to do this."

"I do." He drew a breath. "Just make sure you talk to Reece."

"I will."

"I'm serious, Turco. I'm not using my own wheels."

"I wouldn't want you to."

The VW would probably give out even if they did use it. It wasn't fast enough and the muffler was loud. Grant took a moment before asking about guns.

"I got it covered," Turco said. "I'll handle it." He threw his cigarette over the railing. "That's my deal. I'll handle it. That's my fuckin deal."

Wind blew through the apartment complex and shook the metallic railing. Turco stared down into the courtyard where a green plastic float moved across the pool. He watched the float wander into the deep end of the pool and he put a hand on Grant's shoulder.

The crows broke from the garbage bins and fled into the sky.

When the darkness finally came, it was quick and silent and the town was wholly absorbed in it. The cold, winter silence felt detached from the rest of the wilderness and they left the apartment complex and drove off in the Beetle. Federal Highway was scarce of traffic and the police barriers were gone and the streetlights blinked in cautionary silence. There was night and that was all and it crept across the landscape, coming with no passion or urgency.

7:14 P.M.

The streetlights bled white and shadows crept across vacant bus benches. Harlan watched them pass as they drove by.

The VW's interior was dark, save for a single stereo light glowing around the radio dial. A local talk show discussed the Challenger and the voices were often interrupted by ugly static and there were callers into the show.

Harlan spotted the giant doughnut hanging on the roof of Frosty's Diner. It was made of Plexiglas and Plaster of Paris. Half of it sat torn apart from the tropical storm that August. The donut was brown and white with spray-painted dots for sprinkles. The sight of it made him grin and he said, "Round beach towels."

Grant turned down the stereo. "What?"

"A round beach towel," Harlan said. "I saw the doughnut. I just thought of it."

Turco turned around. "What do you mean?"

"It's round. You don't have to turn it as the sun changes."

"You just change position," Grant said, understanding.

Harlan smiled. "Right."

Grant glanced at Harlan in the rear-view. He nodded.

"You don't have to move the towel," Turco said.

"Yeah."

Turco grinned. "That's not bad, Harlan. That's a good idea."

"I'd buy one," Grant said.

Harlan leaned back into his seat and streetlights flickered across his face and he smiled.

Turco laughed. "Round beach towel."

❀❀❀

Dan Nealey sat behind the Liquor Barn's counter, dressed in plaid button-down and a POW tee shirt hung off his jeans. Hawaii 5-O ran on a small TV, propped up before the sliding window and he kept his leg up on a chair. It had been aching. The painkillers were stale, carrying the chalky aftertaste of rotten antacids.

The glass partition separating his register from the outside drive-thru wore pock marks from bullets. A drunk had tried to rob him last year and he had shot up the glass with a small .25.

Dan had fallen to the floor when the shots rang and a camper had pulled into the drive-thru, scaring the drunk and he fled before he could break the glass and climb into the store. The glass had not shattered and the owner didn't think to replace it anytime soon. Dan fought with the management about replacing the glass. A month later, the diner on Dixie had been robbed. A waitress was killed. Again, Dan threatened to quit and the manager purchased a .33 and a bat. They now sat in a drawer below the register. Dan sometimes kept the pistol tucked into his jacket. He had been issued a similar sidearm in the army and had felt comfortable with it. Older now, less confident about his accuracy, he nevertheless had no doubt he could summon the response. He could fire the gun like he had once done in battle.

He often thought about Libby. How she would go on living if he was shot. She would have problems with the propane tanks on the trailer and she would have to buy double bolts for the door. He wondered if Grant would marry her and they'd move away from this place and find some small patch of land further inland, closer to Orlando or possibly Clearwater.

He thought about this and then he recognized the car's motor a block away. By the time the Volkswagon pulled into the lot, he had put Libby out of his mind and bagged the champagne.

Pulling up to the window, Turco leaned up on Grant's side of the car. He shouted at Dan: "Let's get some service here!"

Dan grinned and turned off the television.

"This place is just packed with customers," Turco said.

"Was til your sorry ass showed up."

Harlan laughed and he kicked Turco's seat and Turco threw a cigarette butt at him.

Dan waved to Grant, looking over the Volkswagon. "The Beetle's looking pretty-titty."

"Washed and waxed," Grant said.

"Making some rumbling over here."

Grant nodded. "Clutch."

"You check the idle?"

"Yeah. I thought it was the cylinders, but then I started stalling at lights."

"Kraut clutches." Dan leaned farther out the drive-thru window. "I believe I do owe somebody a Happy Birthday."

Dan began to sing.

Turco put his hands over his ears and Harlan laughed. They applauded when Dan finished. Drunk kids raced across the parking lot and cussed and Turco gave them the finger and they laughed and ran away.

"I don't think they like my singing," Dan said.

"You're Sinatra," Turco said.

Dan smiled. "Bob Marley here don't like my singing."

"I like it, Dan. It's the best present yet," Grant said.

"Only present," Turco said. He struck a match on the dashboard, throwing it to the wet pavement.

Dan pointed at Turco. "You boys should count your blessings to have a bud like Grant. I know my daughter does."

"I have all kinds'a buds." Turco made a smoke gesture with his hand and Dan shook his head.

"Ain't talking about those buds."

Harlan grinned and Turco stole a cigarette from Grant's pack and he leaned out the window and gave the cigarette to Dan. "Heard the V.A.'s been giving you a shitty time, Mr. Nealey."

Dan struck a match and lit the cigarette. "When you give half your leg to a jungle war, you get bullshit in return."

Harlan nodded.

"Veterans getting shit. Rockets blowing up like soda pop. Reganomics can kiss my ass."

Turco asked about the liquor. "How 'bout stylin' us some MD 40/40. Pronto."

"Ballbuster tonight," Dan said.

"Thirsty ballbuster."

"What are we getting, two bottles?"

"Two bottles. Yes, sir."

Dan looked at Turco. He moved his leg off the chair, slowly.

Grant watched him through the bullet-shot glass, limping in a deliberate pace to the wall cooler. Returning with the bottles, he pointed at Grant. "You ain't drinkin' and drivin'."

"Not at the same time."

"I'm serious."

"No, sir," Grant said. "Pretty much wired on Tylenol and Pepsi. Don't need much else."

"That's good." Dan bagged the liquor and passed the two bottles to Turco. He shrugged off Turco's ten-dollar bill.

"Take it."

"Don't want it." He nodded to Grant. "It's in furtherance of your friend. You got a birthday pass."

Harlan smiled. "Killer. Thanks, Mr. Nearly."

"You take care of Grant. I want my future son-in-law alert 'n responsible. Like Colombo." He faced Turco: "You ever watch Colombo?"

"Yeah, that dog. Take a bite out'a crime and shit."

Dan shook his head. He called Turco an ignorant sonofabitch and handed Grant the champagne.

"What's this?"

"Nothing big," Dan said. "Just a little something for later on, after your shift. Little something for you and Libby and the sunrise."

"Dan, you don't have to-"

"Hey. That's from me. When I give you something, you take it with open arms. Understand?"

Grant smiled and nodded.

"You drink a glass for me," Dan said. "You're only nineteen once, you hear?"

Grant thanked Dan.

"Libby joining you later?"

"Yeah. April from work's driving her over to Todd's."

"Rich boy having a little party?" Dan asked.

"Yeah," Turco said. "And I'm the star attraction."

"You're the star dis traction."

Harlan laughed and Dan asked Grant if Libby had given him his birthday present.

"Not yet."

"You're gonna like it," Dan said.

"I know I will."

Turco shook the liquor, twisting the cap off. He told Grant it was time to leave.

Harlan waved to Dan. "Take care, Mr. Nearly. Thanks a lot."

"Thank Birthday Boy here." He winked at Grant. "Many more to come."

"Thanks for remembering."

Dan nodded and told him anytime.

He watched the VW start off with a thud and roar away. It turned onto Federal Highway and disappeared into a cold, winter drizzle.

When the parking lot was quiet again, Dan went into the back and filled the last of the stock. The television show had ended and a news report came on and there was a woman related to one of the astronauts who had allegedly killed herself. The newswoman said the report couldn't be substantiated and they'd have more information as the story progressed.

Dan shut the TV off and swore at his aching knee.

He downed three pain pills and began counting out the register.

8:10 P.M.

Aldo Bay was a subdivision with guard gates and a private golf course and boardwalks running through manicured patches of pine woods. Todd Hailer's house sat at the end of a cul-de-sac. Christmas lights hung around the garage and the fence was decorated in red ribbons and yards of cotton resembled fake snow.

The party had spread out to the street where beer cans and cigarette butts littered the front lawn and there was Black Sabbath on a living room stereo. Neighbors had complained because the parking was illegal and they'd call a tow truck if the pavement wasn't cleared.

Reece Stanz sat on a yellow and black Ninja 750, adjusting the accelerator. He stood 6'2, trapped in a skinny meth build with long arms that showed tattoo vines the color of moss. A crowd of kids stood around the bike and some had thrown beer cans onto the lawn and Reece told them to pick the shit up.

When Grant's Beetle pulled into the lawn, the muffler discharged a throaty bang, loud as a shotgun. Neighborhood dogs barked. Turco broke from Grant and Harlan, stumbling through the sprinklers, approaching Reece's bike. He inspected a new fearing Reece had installed the Thursday before and he asked if Reece was going to do something about the sissy bar.

"Sissy bar, shit." Reece wiped sweat from his face. "That's the least of my fuckin problems. Still gotta find a clean throttle." He forced the motor and it whined across the lawn. "You hear that shit?"

Turco nodded, drunk. "Cold makes it worse." He told Harlan to pass the liquor. He asked Reece about the clutch.

"Shifting like a sonofabitch."

"Jap bike," Turco said. "What'd you expect?"

"Right?" Reece took a shot of liquor and almost coughed. "Slants couldn't take us down in the Pacific. Had to sabotage the modern sportbike."

Reece spat onto the pavement. He told Turco to clean it up and Turco laughed.

A teen girl moved into Reece's arms. She was wire-thin and had rubber bands for hairbraids and she stared at Harlan.

"You know Cari, right?"

"Yeah," Turco said. "What's up?"

"Not much." She waved to Harlan. Her fingernails were bright purple, the tone of peaked plums. She told Harlan her sister was in one of his classes.

"Mara, right?"

She nodded and passed him back the liquor.

Reece lit a cigarette and asked Turco about the Seminole he had fought on the beach.

"All over town," Turco said, proudly.

"Sure is, brother." Reece asked Turco about the Seminole's surfboard and Turco said that he had snapped the board in two.

"It was piece of shit," Turco said. "Can't trade those boards in for shit."

"Where they get off surfing our shit anyway?"

"No shit, right?"

"Get back to the goddamn reservation." Reece put his arms around Cari's small waist and whispered something about cigarettes.

Cari asked Harlan where Grant was.

"Went inside to look for Libby."

Cari shook her head. "I don't think she's here yet."

"Naw," Reece said, "she's not."

A girl in an OP tee shirt came screaming out the side porch. Her hair was wet with beer and she saw Turco standing in the driveway and whispered something to her friend. She shouted his name and Turco didn't answer and when she moved closer, into the wet sprinkler lawn, Turco finally waved back.

"I'm Lea! You remember me?"

"No."

She pointed to the house's open door and the music from within. "I can't hear you!"

"I said no, I don't fucking remember you!"

Reece laughed.

"Lindsey thinks you're fine!"

"Can she suck the poison out of a python?"

"What?"

"I said, can she suck the poison out of a python?"

The girl stumbled. She called Turco an asshole and started back into the house.

Turco looked at Reece. "Todd's still dating that pig?"

Reece grinned and moved his hand to the back of Cari's waist. "Dude, she's like a moped. Fun to ride til your friends see you on one."

Turco spat out liquor and laughed.

❦❦❦

In the house, there were faces he vaguely recognized. There were light bulbs shaded red and they poured colors over walls and two cats, both white, darted into a hall.

Rush's Working Man was on the living room stereo and a girl with her Jimmy Z shirt unbuttoned danced alone in the kitchen. Kids covered the furniture, their stares fixed on a surf video. Grant recognized one of the surfers from his pool games at Kelly's and asked where Todd was.

"Outside, I think. By the pool."

In the backyard, the crowd was larger, spread out. The pool light was a turquoise glow and the water appeared cold, solid as stone in the dark and through the sliding glass doors, Grant could see small blades of grass and dead insects floating on its surface.

Stepping onto the patio deck, he saw Marco from Sebastian Inlet, standing alone, pouring himself beer at the keg. He moved over to him and asked him if the tap was fresh.

"Fresh as piss water." Marco blew foam off his cup. "Least it's free, right?"

Grant nodded and studied the crowd that hugged the ends of the pool. A neighbor's dog jumped a fence and was roaming around the backyard. A boy tried to feed her beer and Marco told the boy to piss off and he shouted at the dog and slapped his hands and the dog left them.

Marco turned back to Grant and asked where Libby was.

"Still at work, I guess."

"Turco and Harlan here?"

Grant nodded. "Yeah, wasted somewhere."

Marco slurped his beer. "Pretty wasted myself."

"Off that shit?"

Marco wiped beer from his chin and grinned and his eyes shined in the heavy porch light. "Naw, bro. Pretty much peakin' on some low-grade airplane. Shit's looking all kinds'a insane." He stared at the pool deck's wooden beams and reached into his shirt pocket. "Wanna drop, man?"

Grant shook his head. He told Marco he had to work.

"Dude, you could work ten times more radical on the shit I'm on."

Grant's head was throbbing and he closed his eyes. He asked Marco where Todd was.

Marco pointed to a table where a single candle flickered. "Right over there, bro."

Todd Hailer sat at a patio table far away from the pool. A net of hair covered his face and his eyed were fixated on a lone candle in the center. He was sick and an empty bottle of NyQuil cough medicine sat on the table.

A girl sat beside him, drinking rum from a Cape Canaveral souvenir cup and she stared at the NyQuil bottle. She giggled when the candle flickered.

The girl waved at Grant. "It's the Birthday Boy."

Grant nodded. He had forgotten the girl's name and he put a hand out to Todd. "Todd, what's up?"

Todd sat still, staring at the candle. Cough medicine from the NyQuil bottle had spilled over, creeping into a stream that ran over the table's edge, onto the Chattahoochee patio floor. It was a green swirl, glowing in the candlelight.

Someone yelled shit and kids laughed.

Todd watched the flame.

The girl giggled. She put the cup down and took Grant's hand. "Todd's somewhere else, you know?" She gave Grant the souvenir cup filled with rum.

Grant shrugged.

"C'mon." She rubbed Grant's wrist. "You'll like it. Promise." She blinked and mumbled something out the side of her mouth and Grant couldn't understand. She motioned to the cup and Grant took a sip. She giggled and he took another sip. She arched back, putting one leg onto the patio seat, small enough to expose the stitching of her yellow panties. She told Grant the pool light was warm.

A skinhead broke from the house, carrying one of the two cats in his arms. The cat scratched and whined and the skinhead shouted something about Mexicans and jumped into the pool.

The girl laughed and whispered to Todd and Todd didn't answer. The cat bucked and scrambled and it swam to the pool's edge.

🐦🐦🐦

"It's got a self-loading chamber." Reece aimed the .25 at the bedroom's wall and Turco studied the gun. "Distance is for shit, but it packs some hardcore close-range."

He gave the gun to Turco and Turco gripped the butt of the firearm with his left hand. He had held it many times before and seemed all the more impressed with its action. It was lighter than he had remembered. He owned toy guns with more weight.

Sitting on the edge of the waterbed, he aimed into the carpet and imagined a well and he asked about the nine millimeter.

Reece paused. He reached into his jacket and produced the Brac nine-millimeter. "This is a six-bill gun, Turk." He smacked out the live clip, rendering the gun safe and flipped it out to Turco, who took it eagerly. He put his finger through the trigger hole. "Might need it all up front."

Turco inspected the chamber. He aimed the gun at a poster of The Clash and said something about money and Reece lit a cigarette.

"I didn't get that," Reece said.

"I can give you a hundred now and double tomorrow." Turco pulled the trigger and the gun made a click. "That's twelve hundred in your pocket."

"How do I know I'm goddamn getting it tomorrow?"

Turco thought about that, then he pulled something gold and thin from his jeans pocket and it glittered like piano keys in the dim glow of the bedroom nightlight. It was the necklace he had purchased from Mars Bohr earlier that morning on the pier.

Reece went quiet at the sight of it. He took it in his hand and felt the weight of the gold. He put the necklace up to the nightlight and studied the small indentations in the chain. "What's this?"

"Mayan. Know anything about 'em?"

Reece shrugged. He inspected a charm attached on the chain. A dolphin with diamond eyes was jumping a wave, suspended forever in the action.

Reece bit the gold. "What is this?"

"Insurance." Turco pulled back the nine-millimeter's slide bolt and fired a dry clip.

🐦🐦🐦

Cari kept a pillow on the lap of her skirt. Her skin was warm, smooth cotton against Harlan's face and when he'd move around she'd giggle and play with his hair. In the glow of the TV, she was beautiful, smelling of bubble gum and Charlie perfume. They talked about high school. She was failing English and she'd have take summer school. She lived in the same trailer park as Libby. She'd practice baton on her lawn.

A surf video of Tom Curren played on the big screen television and kids no older than sixteen passed around a plastic bong and drank warm beer and they hollered and a surfer on TV caught a wave. Cari asked Harlan if the surfer was Tom Curren.

Harlan nodded. "The guy can't be stopped."

"I like his hair."

"Nobody gives a shit about his hair."

"That's not true."

Harlan grinned and Cari touched a strand of his hair.

Turco walked into the room, brown paper bag in hand. He called Tom Curren a faggot and spit on the television. Reece stood beside Turco, cracking open a beer. He laughed when Turco jumped over the couch.

"Fuck him, fuck Thompson! Fuck the Slaters!"

Reece hollered and he threw his beer to the carpet. "My boy, Turco!"

"Goddamn straight."

A boy with chin stubble, chewing tobacco looked up at Turco from the living-room recliner. He recognized Turco from the beach. "You're Brian Turcorelli?"

"The one and only, none so holy."

The boy nodded and grinned. "Vay's looking for you." He sparked the lighter.

Turco's grin drained.

The boy asked for the bong.

Turco suddenly sprang from the couch, slamming into the boy. Clutching the butt of the bagged 9mm, Turco hammered the boy in the face and blood erupted from his broken nose. Bodies scattered as Turco fell upon the bleeding body.

He struck his face again and the paper bag broke. He grabbed the bong off the floor, smashing it over the boy's head. Plastic tore his eye and a girl ran out into the kitchen hallway.

"Shit!" The boy coughed blood and Turco hit him again and his knuckled were red and cut. He then grabbed an astray and broke it across the boy's face.

The boy's cheeks filled with blood.

"Bitch!" Turco shouted. "I'm looking for you!"

The boy began to convulse. More ceramic glass filled his face and his mouth flooded with blood and he fought to speak. He screamed a girl's name and someone went to get her.

Turco stuffed the broken shards of the ashtray into the boy's mouth and he cursed the blood. "Looking for you!"

Reece grabbed Turco, pulling him back from the shattered coffee table. He grinned and called Turco Rocky and wiped the blood from his shoulders.

The surfing video played.

Turco clutched the brown paper bag. He washed liquor around in his mouth and spat it onto the boy and he told the boy he was invincible.

Reece laughed.

"Fucking invincible!"

✿✿✿

On the side of the house, hidden among lawn sprinklers, Turco cleaned his body of the blood. In the driveway, a pack of girls cried and one motioned to Turco and began cussing and her friend pulled her over to the street and she wiped mascara from her eyes.

Turco threw his stained shirt to the lawn, cursing the asshole for bleeding all over it. The liquor sat in his stomach, aching; dead weight like so many coins. He pulled a sprinkler head loose and threw it onto the street and he saw Grant charging through the grass and started toward him. "Dude, where you been-"

Grant screamed, grabbing Turco, throwing him up against the side of the house. "What are you, a psychotic?!" He shook Turco. "You crack open the kid's skull?!"

"Get your hands off me-"

"You nearly waste the kid cause he mentions somebody's name?!"

Turco screamed and threw himself back onto Grant. He told Grant to fuck off.

Grant forced him back against the wall again. "The guy's having a fucking seizure!"

"Goddamn it!" Turco spat into the grass. "Get your hands off me!"

Grant pressed his weight against Turco. He finally let go, heading off through the cold sprinklers and a surge of police lights swept across the wet grass and a kid was thrown onto the back of a car and handcuffed.

Turco followed Grant through the lawn, both of them keeping distance from the police lights. "The kook was talking shit!"

"So you nearly waste him?"

"Hold up, man."

"Fuck you, Turco."

"Hold up!"

Turco gripped Grant's shoulder, digging fingernails into skin. They stared at one another.

Turco said: "If I wanted to waste that bitch, I'd have used this." He held up the wet paper bag, exposing to Grant the contours of the Brac 9mm.

Grant gazed at the weapon for a moment. He pushed through Turco, starting back to his Beetle and The Police played from a radio.

"Grant, where you going?"

Grant said nothing and Turco asked again and a Doberman leapt onto a fence and barked and began tearing at the fencing with its teeth.

Turco shouted this time. "I asked you where you're going?!"

"That's it," Grant said. "It's over."

"The hell it is." Turco raced up in front of Grant, holding out a set of car keys. "C'mon, I got his car."

Grant stopped and stared at the keys. The metal was tinged in blood. "Those are Todd's."

"Todd ain't in no condition to drive. Besides, you didn't wanna use your own wheels, remember?"

"What about Reece?"

"What about him."

"You said Reece was in on this."

"Grant, we don't have time for this shit, are you on this or what?"

Grant looked at him but didn't answer.

A police siren wailed from a block away and lights flashed across the lawn. Two deputy patrols came around the corner, road-blocking the street. Kids broke from the house. Neighbors stood on porches, arms crossed, watching police cars. The Doberman had jumped the gate and was going through trash on the curb.

Turco saw Harlan coming out the front door, Cari at his side. They froze in the flood of bodies scrambling from the police.

Turco put a hand on Grant's arm. "Look. We gotta move."

A yellow glow fell around the pavement, mixing with the red and blue police lights. The glow warped and bled like paint.

Grant realized it was the acid he had sipped. There was a pulse sound, then distortion and then nearby conversations began to ebb and flow.

His Volkswagon Beetle was trapped in the new wave of vehicles fighting to leave the cul-de-sac. He could make out the edges of the shuttle smoke hovering above the neighborhood and it glowed, radiating colors. He felt exposed in it and it clung to the sky. There were no longer places he could hide. It was darker than any night he could recall and it felt that day would never surface and there were parts of the moon that showed themselves through the clouds but that was all.

The smoke cloud was part of the sky now, outstretched tentacles of gas and particle.

Cops ran from their cars and began chasing kids.

A drunk teenager threw a bottle and Grant stood on the grass and stared into the smoke cloud.

"C'mon!" Turco shouted. "The car's parked around back!"

Turco called to Harlan and he shouted something back. His words were lost in police siren.

"Now!" Turco shouted. "Let's go!"

Harlan hesitated and he said something to Cari. She pulled him back and began to cry. Harlan whispered to her.

"Fuck her! Let's go!"

Harlan kissed Cari. He told her that he'd be back and he ran around the crowds and into the wet lawn.

Turco turned to Grant, gesturing to the second garage around back. "C'mon. Thirty minutes and it's all over."

Grant stood there a moment, wet and trembling. He stared at the flood lights hanging over the house's corner. They were twisting, bending. He glanced at his watch.

9:45

Harlan ducked through the lawn sprinklers, shielding his notebook. He followed Grant and Turco around the side of the house.

Moments later, a green 1978 Chevy Nova crept out from the darkness, onto the street behind Todd Hailer's house. The headlights powered on and the engine rumbled, choking to life.

Turco adjusted the side mirror. No police had followed them.

Grant and Harlan kept silent in the car; their breath visible in the night cold. Tract homes showed dark windows and lawn sprinklers were on and mailboxes dressed like candy canes reflected off the Nova's headlights. Christmas lights lingered on roofs, blinking red and green.

Grant gasped breaths. He saw his mother in the hospital bed and there was a hallway.

Harlan stared at a mailbox covered in candy-cane wrapping. He whispered the name Ramsel on the box.

Turco put the wipers on and he turned the corner and drove out of the subdivision.

❀❀❀

She left the Winn-Dixie with April somewhere after 8:30 and the roads had become clear and they spoke nothing of the crowds or of the shuttle. She had wished that she had called Grant at his apartment but it was too late now. There was that dream that she continued to think about but she told no one of it, not even herself and it was like a weight pressed into her mind. The winos from the liquor store and neighboring pub stood drunk in the parking lot and they shouted something to them and Libby ignored them. The rain had stopped and they climbed into the Honda and Libby began to sob.

April asked what was wrong and Libby shook her head and said it was nothing and that the party was in Alto Bay, but April already knew this. Libby apologized and April said it was no problem and the car started out onto the long stretch of Federal Highway. She glanced past the windshield, into the dark night, hoping to see past the fragment of the shuttle cloud; hoping to see something more and perhaps gaze upon stars but there were no stars and the new rain had brought with it a grey mist that utterly canvassed the sky. Libby put a hand on her lap and she could feel the contours of the bump and it made her want to cry again and that's when she saw a speck of crows lined like black beads of an abacus on the telephone wire.

❦❦❦

He vomited on the side of Dixie Highway, not far from a K-Mart parking lot. His Firebird sat in the dirt, headlights dim, predatory. He wiped his face and drank the remaining liquor.

The crippled vet at the Liquor Barn never checked ID.

The cripple was closing the store when he pulled up to the window and the cripple was happy enough to sell him the liquor.

He spotted crows circling the beach. He had watched the crows many times before and he knew they would stay all night and wait for scraps left from the winos.

The gun was in the glove compartment. It belonged to his brother. He had stolen it three days ago from the shed behind their trailer. It felt heavier, looked blacker than it ever had and sweat saturated its steel handle and the metal smelled of rusted carnival rides. Sitting alone in the Firebird, radio belching static, he thought of nailing the accelerator, driving the car into the marsh just across the pavement. The cold and pain and the chill of the marsh water would shatter his drunk mind and he would drown and it would be slow. He would feel the water in his throat and it would feel like it had earlier that day at the beach but there was still more to do so he continued to drink and watch the road.

He thought of his father's death. The car crashed along the roadside. The blood dried on the windshield. Standing as a boy on the road. A wash of light. Blacks and reds. There was a news van.

His brother had cursed it and the gun had stuck to the old man's fingers and his brother was crying.

He stared out to A1A, watching a smear of headlights come and pass. There was a convoy of trucks and a station wagon and then there was a green, glimmering Chevy Nova. In a flash, he saw his sunburned face behind the wheel, his bleached, knotted hair a tangled spider's web. The eyes blue and crystallized that made him think of storms when the sky grew dark.

He suddenly felt light and he was longer pulled down by the weight of the liquor. Although his face was filled with warm red, it was cold and he knew that the blood was rage and it felt as good as anything he had ever experienced.

The Nova's battered engine wheezed and gurgled and the sound disintegrated in the ocean wind.

He threw up again. He started the Firebird's ignition and screamed. He could see the Nova in the dark as he spun his brother's car back onto the highway.

❂❂❂

Turco lit the cigarette, burning matches into the wind. His eyes stayed focused on A1A and the passing slabs of white from the streetlights. Slouched in the Nova's passenger's seat, Grant wiped a new film of sweat from off his face. The throbbing pain had returned, stretching down to parts of his throat and stomach; a twisting, jagged pain. Colors and sounds fired around the car and they were soulless forms with no beginning or end.

"What is it?" Turco asked.

Grant swallowed, as though struggling to speak. "Rum. Rum was spiked." He coughed. "Starting to peak."

The Nova's engine grinded and churned.

"Ride it out."

"Can't do this."

"You can."

"Turn it around. The car."

Turco said nothing.

"Turn it around, Turk."

"Almost over."

"It's not."

"It is."

"Turco."

"It's almost over."

Grant found the door handle and rolled down the window and the air was cool. He pressed his face up against the glass and found the smoke cloud in the dark; its dissipated trail following like a shy stray.

"Let me see the daylight," he whispered. He coughed and forced back vomit. "I want to see the daylight."

Harlan spotted the red light they were racing towards, just before the Trackston Avenue intersection. He tried to speak but froze. He whispered at Turco to slow down.

Turco punched the gas and fired the Nova through the red light. Horns blared and colors flashed by him and he kept his stare straight. A homeless couple was crossing the street and the man kicked the car's side. The woman cussed and the rusted shopping cart fell and cans and glass bottles spilled over.

Harlan watched them dissolve away.

Two traffic lights later, Turco pulled the brown paper bag up from the floorboard.

Harlan leaned up to the front seat, his face pale. He shouted Turco's name.

Turco turned down the stereo and threw his cigarette into the rain.

Harlan asked where they were going.

Turco chewed and swallowed a piece of tobacco residue. He told Harlan about the Save-It-All and that they needed beer.

"Thought we were gonna get a piece of the shuttle?"

"We gotta get some beer first."

Harlan wiped sweat and spit from his chin. He swallowed a dry breath and said that he didn't feel like drinking anymore.

"Maybe I do," Turco said.

Harlan looked out the back window. Rain beads crept down the glass and he put his face to the glass and felt the cold. His hands were shaking and he turned to Grant, sprawled along the side of the passenger door. "You okay?"

Grant closed his eyes. He saw swirls of black water and thought about pool light and the colors in a dream then he opened his eyes and Libby was standing in empty aisles of the supermarket. There was a hospital bed.

"Grant?"

Grant swallowed and coughed. He took a deep breath. He told Harlan that he was cool.

10:20 P.M.

Libby broke from April Shay's Honda before it could pull up to the house. Sprinklers were shattered over Todd Hailer's lawn and the grass carried a stream of running muck into the street. The boy Turco had beaten was being handled into the back of an ambulance and a mask covered in plastic tubes was set over his bruised face.

Libby was pushed off to the side by police and she watched the ambulance fight its way through the surge. Sirens were loud and she didn't hear her name being shouted across the lawn.

Cari shouted it again and Libby turned and saw her standing beside the driveway. The girl was the sister of Mara Wells. She waved Libby over to a dry patch of lawn where she stood with Reece and she told Libby that Grant was looking for her.

"Where is he?"

Cari took Libby's hand and tears ran down her face and her sneakers were soaked from the wet lawn and she smelled of beer. "The cops. They're looking for them."

"What?"

Cari wiped tears away with her arm. "Turco beat some kid up. They drove off in Todd's car."

Libby looked at Reece. He sat on his Ninja, arms crossed, watching cops. He flicked a cigarette at a police sedan. "Assholes." He spat on the lawn and checked the side of his bike. "Nothing to fucking do but this shit."

"Where are they?"

Reece turned to Libby as though she had just arrived beside him. "Who?"

"Grant! Turco!"

Reece swore and spit again. He rubbed stubble on his face and told Cari to get on the bike.

"I don't want to. I want to go home."

"I'm goddamn taking you home, you stupid bitch!"

"Don't call me a bitch!"

"Just get on the fucking bike!"

"No!"

She fled back into the house and Libby asked again where Grant was.

Reece shook his head. "Libby, don't worry about it-"

"Where are they, you motherfucker?!"

10:30 P.M.

The Chevy Nova turned off the long strip of A1A, crawling into the Save-It-All. The parking lot was wet from rain and trash skirted across the pavement and found the ends of dirt patches.

From the Nova's windshield, Turco spotted the manager's Toyota Cressida, parked before the doors. He could see an air freshener in the shape of a cherry strung to its dashboard. He told Grant and Harlan to roll up the windows and make sure the back doors were locked and he put the Nova into a hard reverse and pointed the headlights to the highway and the engine fell to a low rumble.

Glancing at his watch, he picked up the brown paper bag. He looked at Harlan in the rear view mirror. "When we get out, climb into the driver's seat."

"Me?"

"Yeah. Keep the engine running. Be ready to go."

Harlan's eyes swelled and he coughed and stuttered. "I'm gonna drive, Turk?"

Turco nudged Grant. "Let's go."

Harlan asked Turco what was going on.

"Don't worry about it." Sweat poured down from Turco's hair, filling his face. "Just get in the front of the car."

A tear crept down Harlan's cheek and he was trembling from the cold and he looked to Grant and said his name.

A truck roared by on the highway and tires peeled across the wet slick of rain.

Grant fought through the acid flashes and everything bent and split and the truck was still in his mind and he had a vision of the headlights filling his face. He focused on the strong light in the convenience store, stitched together and breathing.

Harlan said his name again and Grant put a hand out to him. "It's okay, Harlan. We'll be right back." He swallowed breath. "Keep… keep your eyes on the road." He threw open the door, stumbling out of the car and onto the pavement.

Turco sprung from the driver's side, slamming the door shut.

Alone in the car, Harlan watched them start for the store. He choked back a new rush of nausea, trembling, eyes red. He fell into the front seat, behind the wheel. Rolling up the black-tinted windows, Harlan was suddenly engulfed in shadows. The darkness filled his face and when he looked in the rearview, he couldn't see himself.

The car rumbled and belched.

He kept his foot on the accelerator, tapping the gas to keep the engine alive. He tapped it to make sure he was still there, sitting in the driver's seat. He clicked on the panel light. He opened his spiral notebook to the page of Grant's birthday poem and his hand shook.

Approaching the store's entrance, Turco glanced again at his watch. Adrenaline poured up into his throat and his body trembled and each muscle in his arm felt heavy; the blood in his wrists, neck pulsing. The feeling was unnatural.

Grant stumbled in the drizzle, fluorescent light filling his eyes. "This is bad," he muttered. "This is so bad." He said it again, deep in his mind and began to think of Libby. He saw her crying in her car.

Turco pulled the Raven .25 from the paper bag, practically forcing it into Grant's hand. He wiped rain onto his wet jeans and told Grant to keep the gun on the guy at the counter. "The fucker doesn't move an inch."

"The counter guy."

"That's what I said." Turco pulled the black ski masks from the bag.

🌀🌀🌀

Blasting through the front door, mask covering his face, Grant was instantly overcome by the icy fluorescents. The cold wall of air conditioning. The gun in his hand and the cheap wool of mask filling his face.

Turco ripped out the 9mm, waving it at the aisles of groceries and magazines. He screamed into the store: "Everybody! On the floor!"

Two boys stood at the magazine rack, skateboards clung to their sides. Turco recognized them as the boys he'd sold dope to on Main Street earlier that morning and he couldn't remember their names and they stood frozen, paralyzed by the sight of the gun. One dropped his skateboard and went to pick it up.

Turco screamed to hit the ground.

They dropped to the cold floor and put their hands out on the linoleum.

A man wearing a NASA security uniform clutched a newspaper and stood beside the beer cooler. He flinched when Turco flashed the gun.

"You deaf? On the fucking floor!"

The man nodded and he lowered himself to the cold linoleum. He left the cooler door open and beer cans rolled from the bottom shelf, spilling to the floor and the grind and churn of the freezer fan filled the store.

A paper-thin counter employee started for the floor.

Turco whipped the gun on his face. "Not you, asshole. Back against the wall." He gestured with the gun. "The wall!"

"Which wall?"

Turco jumped the counter, tripping over the roll of daily register receipts. He caught himself, grabbing the employee, pressing the gun up to his head. "The one right behind you!"

A voice cried out from the back room and Grant could only make out the word *hello*.

Turco kicked over a grocery bag station and he cussed and kicked them again and the plastic bags flew across the air like limp party balloons.

The counter employee fell against the wall and mumbled a prayer.

A voice from the back room: "Hello?"

"Freeze back there, cocksucker!" Turco put the weapon on the closed door. "Back room! On the motherfuckin floor!"

"Okay, sir."

"I'll blow heads off."

"Okay." An African drawl; soothing, polite. "I'm on the floor."

Turco glanced at Grant. He was clinging to a postcard fixture; half-aiming, struggling within the heavy acid peak and he couldn't find Turco.

"Get that piece on the guy!"

Grant forced his arm back into a steady aim and the warped, bubbling vision of the counter employee stuck to the wall with arms out to his side and he appeared to Grant as a flailing insect form.

Turco whipped back to the man in the NASA guard uniform, his body trembling, cold beside the open beer cooler.

"You! NASA!" He gestured to the man's belt. "Slide your gun over here."

"I don't have a gun."

Turco fired off a round above the man's head and glass splintered and fell in the beer cooler's door. A twelve pack of beer had been shot and beer fizzled across the floor. The two boys covered their heads and Turco saw that the taller one was crying.

"Shut the hell up!"

"I'm sorry."

"Don't be fuckin sorry, just don't cry."

"I can't help it!"

Turco's eyes poured through the ski mask. Again, he aimed the gun on the NASA security guard. "Get up, go to the front!"

"My friend, I ain't gonna do shit."

"I didn't say do shit, I said get up here!"

"I have a boy about your age."

"I don't give a fuck, get up here!"

The man nodded, sweat pouring through his uniform. He began to rise from the cold floor.

"No, asshole. Crawl."

"Okay."

"Now!"

The man got to his knees and began a slow, clumsy crawl through the candy and snacks. The store colors washed through Grant and he heard Turco tell him something and he nodded. He kept the gun on the counter employee.

Reaching the front counter, the man kept his hands flat on the floor and mumbled something about his boy and Turco told him to shut up.

Turco gestured to Grant. "Keep that gun on them. Anyone moves, you open up."

"Yeah."

"I'm serious, you fucking unload."

"Yeah! Just get the shit already!"

Turco scratched an itch through the ski mask wool and turned to a closed door that was marked Employees Only and he could hear the man breathing from the other side of the door. Reaching underneath the counter, he pressed a button that sent the lock open. He faced the counter employee and almost grinned because he felt proud. "I've been watching, asshole." He put the gun on the young man's face and told him that if he'd move more than three inches, he'd be shot in the face and he'd still be alive. The employee nodded and Turco moved past the employee and through the door.

In the back room, an Ethiopian man wearing a Miami Dolphins tee shirt and brown jeans was lying face-down on the ground. The man kept a metal box visible at his side.

"That for me?"

The man said nothing.

Turco kicked a Bud Light Superbowl display at the man. He put the gun to his head and the man began to wheeze. He clutched a plastic inhalator and Turco told him to drop it to the ground.

The man pleaded and Turco put the gun to his head and he knew that the man was the store's assistant manager. He drove a Toyota Cressida and had once thrown a cigarette at Turco when he skated too close to his car. He had called the police when the kids smoked dope.

"You put that shit down!" Turco shouted.

"It helps me breathe."

"You wanna breathe right now?"

"Yes, I do."

"Then you drop that fucking thing and do what I say!"

The man nodded and carefully set the inhalator on the floor and Turco shouted at him to open the safe.

"It's not a safe."

Turco kicked him and the man fell back to the ground but didn't scream. The inhalator rolled a few inches on the floor and he kept his grip on the metal box.

Turco buried the 9mm's muzzle into the man's head. "You feel that?"

"Yes."

"Feel that?"

"I do."

"Open the goddamn safe."

The man nodded, keeping his hands exposed. He moved over to the small safe. He pulled the safe's handle and opened the door to reveal the interior of a miniature fridge. Turco threw the man to the side and looked into the safe and saw a six pack of Pepsi. There were two brown paper bags; one of them stained from a rotting banana.

He stood frozen and there was a moment where he almost grinned. "The fuck is this?"

The man whispered in Ethiopian.

"English, cocksucker!"

"Lunches. My employees' lunches."

Turco screamed and struck the man with the butt of the gun. The man fell to the ground, cradling his head. A trickle of blood bubbled from his skull.

Turco kicked the metal box out from under the man's arm. The lid flipped open and there were pornographic magazines in the box and video tapes and a list of phone numbers.

Turco began to cry. "What is this?!"

"Don't kill me."

Turco screamed.

He kicked the man.

Grant could hear Turco shouting through the closed office door. His voice, amplified, vicious.

The second voice screamed through the wall: "There isn't a safe! Sir, we don't have no safe!"

The voice was followed by the deep, buffered sound of a kick.

Grant fell back against the store's widows and he struggled to keep the Raven .25 aimed on the counter. He shouted to Turco if everything was all right and he could make out Turco's cursing and shouting, the sound of rummaging, things on walls ripping down. A glass mirror shattered; gun half-raised, sinking in his hand with the weight of a brick.

The two boys sat still under the long aisle of magazines and the man in the NASA guard uniform lay in a puddle of cold water that ran from the open cooler door.

Grant shouted: "What the fuck is going on back there?!"

Silence answered and facing the counter, Grant suddenly spotted a circular rack in the corner. Clung on its metallic branches hung bright, round beach towels the size of bed sheets. Tanning lotions and sundries surrounded the display.

Grant looked at them and grinned and for a moment, the distortion and nausea left him and the towels were as yellow as bright sunlight and he began to laugh.

"Round beach towels." He pulled off the black ski mask and scratched his face. He grinned again. "Harlan's beach towels!"

Grant went to touch them and that's when the dark blue Firebird pulled into the lot.

🌍🌍🌍

Alone in the driver's seat of the Nova, face hovering over a spiral-bound notebook, Harlan muttered words and phrases as fast as thoughts.

A lone panel light shined down over his brown strands of hair and the shadows on his face, twisting and hallucinogenic, gave his cheeks the thin form of a starving child. The blue in his eyes was drained from the light and darkness poured around him.

His pen hand trembled and there were splotches of ink over the paper; the scribbling clumsy, butchered.

The crane in the sand at the Westerfield condo site.

Yellow and rusted against the sky.

He muttered something he could barely hear through the rumbling of car engine. Words over the page:

Yours is ocean

Out of the tumble.

That strides for sense of sight

That finds itself in cold water's depths,

Fills some form. That bares all, settles in sleep.

Harlan crossed out words and saw the morning.

The crane overtaken by the night tides. Drowning in dark water. Yellow peak still visible amid the crest of waves.

Periods and commas, simple and straight, trading like currency across the page.

The marijuana sent his skin into cold, numb clumps of matter.

The crane swallowed whole by ocean.

He scribbled the final words onto the page:

Grant's Ocean

The tall, slender form climbed out the Firebird, marching through the headlights, approaching the driver's side of the Nova. The gun pulled from the back of the belt buckle. Tears filling his face. He aimed at the window.

Harlan studied the finished page. He muttered the poem and he thought of Cari. Her breath against his skin. The waxy slick of lipstick.

He gently tore the page loose.

He felt the shadow above him and turned into the driver's window. He saw the Seminole's face and thought about the ocean water and watched the gun fire.

❧❧❧

A pop, deafening and crisp, shot through the air. Grant could see the tall, shirtless form of the Seminole firing a second shot into the car. A white flash of light accompanied the gun's discharge.

He stood motionless in the store, gun hanging at the tip of his finger. He whispered Harlan's name and saw the blood sprayed over the side of the Nova.

❧❧❧

At the next round of gunfire, Turco dropped the metal box. He rushed to open the door and the bolt was locked. He screamed Grant's name and kicked the door. He could hear the two boys crying from the store aisles and he began to cuss and he smashed the door with the weight of his body and screamed.

"You have to punch 221," the Ethiopian muttered, clutching his bleeding head.

Cursing, gun in hand, Turco fumbled the code. More gunshots sounded off, consuming every inch of space.

"Goddamn door!" Turco punched in the code again.

"221."

Turco aimed and fired and a click rang out. He kicked the door open, charging into the store. Eyes filled with sweat, he could barely see Grant standing numbly before the store's shattered windows, trading gunfire with the form he recognized as the Seminole.

Turco screamed Grant's name and the boys cried.

Grant fired rounds, the gun always straight, an extension of his arm.

The Seminole's gunfire ripped apart the magazine racks behind Grant. The boys screamed, cradling their hands over their heads.

Turco leapt over the register counter, throwing the ski mask to the floor. "What in Christ?"

Grant continued to fire the gun.

"Grant!"

A new shot fired and Turco felt pressure; the impact of a metal rod. The feeling splintered over his chest like breaking pieces of glass and he felt himself projected into air. He fell back onto a magazine rack and open space filled his chest and warm blood slick went over his clothes.

The man lying at the beer cooler shot another into Turco's throat, armed with a small ankle piece hidden underneath his pants leg.

Deep blood poured down Turco's neck and his lungs crushed. Drowning in open air, he stared at the security guard and fired back.

The beer cooler shattered. A second shot struck the man's face and blood ran and he slapped to the floor like a piece of wood slate.

Turco dropped the 9mm, crashing back into the rack of beach towels and he suddenly saw morning.

The British couple he had photographed.

How many pictures of himself were tucked away in the background of strangers?

The pier.

The orange juice he'd tasted.

His brother sitting in his wheelchair and a boy he had once played a card game with when he was a child. Aisles in a department store ten minutes before closing and becoming lost in them.

His father on the far end of the rock jetty and he went to him.

❦❦❦

Grant fired his last round and a bullet struck the Seminole above the waist. He screamed and dropped the gun and he called Grant a bastard and began to limp back to the Firebird's open door, leaking blood.

Grant fell out the shattered doors, stumbling into the parking lot. He fired the gun but they were dry clicks. His index finger, blistered from the trigger, finally set loose the .25.

Struggling, glass buried in his skin, he limped through the rain puddles. He screamed at the Seminole.

The Firebird found the highway, burning out. Red tail lights stung the darkness and Grant saw them as eyes.

The scream of police siren rose in the air and a Sheriff's deputy took chase.

The Firebird spun off the road and crashed into granite rock hugging the dark jetty. Its front instantly pressed in like a paper accordion, oozing smoke and oil.

A smashed horn whined and police chatter rippled through the air and more sedans converged.

Grant limped up to the side of the Chevy Nova, staring into the blown-out driver's window. Blood covered his notebook and body. The dashboard was filled with glass shards.

Grant fell to the side of the car.

Blood ran from his stomach, drenching his jeans.

He slid down the side of the Chevy Nova and he took deep breaths and it was cold. He could make out the dying silhouette of rocket smoke filling the apex, diminished now, hanging low and shapeless. It barely lingered, struggling to remain whole. Grant knew by dawn, it would be gone.

His face had gone numb and there was no pain.

The Seminole screamed. There was a blood slick on the Firebird and someone had a flashlight and a police siren fell dead.

Grant whispered Libby's name and cradled up against the side of the car and put his hands on his chest.

He saw the shuttle floating in space.

He was holding her and it felt like years.

January 27th
1:20 p.m.

Libby walked out from the Nation Beach Hallmark, crisp white paper gift bag in her hand.

A little girl, dressed in a plain church dress with rose-red pigtails, had watched her come out and Libby had the urge to walk back into the store and buy a piece of candy for the girl but the girl was already gone, swept up by her mother and taken into the supermarket.

Libby met Turco and Harlan at the bus bench and Harlan saw the bag in her hand. "Let's see it."

"Don't get your paws all over it." She reached into the bag, producing a small, white jewelry box the shape of a sea shell.

Flipping the box open, Turco studied the small, silver dolphin necklace charm that sat on a pillow of red velvet, glistening silver, reflecting in the afternoon light. Glowing auras orbited around the metal; an illusion made from mid-morning sunlight.

Harlan smiled.

Libby gestured to the dolphin's tiny, glittering eye. "See? Those are three diamonds in the eye."

"One for each of us," Harlan said.

Libby smiled. "That's right." Her eyes were soft gray; Irish fieldstone.

Turco carefully took the jewelry box in hand and inspected the charm. He nodded and told her that it was pretty nice.

"It's simple, right?"

"It's all Grant."

Libby's face went bright and she smiled. "You think?"

"Libby, he's gonna love it." Turco passed it to Harlan. "You better write something to go with it. A poem or somethin."

Harlan studied the three diamonds that made up the dolphin's eye. He nodded and told them that he would and Turco lit a new cigarette.

Libby asked Turco if he had picked out the necklace.

"No." His eyes pierced at the sunlight filling the strip mall's lot. "I pick it up tomorrow."

"Make sure it fits the charm."

"I know."

"It has to fit through this hole."

"Libby, I know." Turco muttered something about the pier and threw the cigarette to the pavement.

Libby took the jewelry box from Harlan and gave it to Turco. She huddled because it was cold and there were breezes off the highway and they blew the red and blue flags of the used car dealer around like cards on bicycle wheels. She said, "I want to give it to him tomorrow night." She pointed at Turco.

Turco nodded and smacked the box shut and stuffed it into the deep of his jeans and took a drag of his cigarette. "I never knew Grant had a thing for dolphins."

"He loves them," Libby said. "Dolphins are man's best friend."

JANUARY 28TH
11:36 A.M.

Rusty Vay crept out from the condo's parking lot, onto the dock that stretched into the shallow water of Westerfield Sound. He had taken the shortcut through the construction yards and his legs were covered in dirt and erosion. He was clear of the pylons now and the launch pad was visible, rising up two miles away, stretching high and straight into the sky.

The shuttle was perched upright.

He believed it was just about the tallest thing he had ever seen.

He found Harlan sitting alone at the dock's edge, huddled in his backpack and surf parka, struggling to light the tip of a joint. Rusty could see the weed was dry and stale. It stunk up the January air and Rusty made a face when a trail of smoke blew by him.

"I knew you'd be here," Rusty said. "Couldn't wait to light that shit."

"It's pretty stale, I gotta admit."

"Turco weed. What'd you expect?"

Harlan took another hit of the joint and passed it to Vay. He kept the spiral-bound notebook safely underneath his arm and Rusty winced and took a drag of the marijuana. He gestured to the launch pillars and exhaled pot. "They sending that up today or what?"

"Yeah," Harlan said. "Forty seconds and counting." He glanced at his watch. "Thirty five."

Rusty fell down beside Harlan and belched. The marijuana ran through his body. He cradled the joint from the strong ocean window.

A wave hit the side of the dock, shifting wood around like the keys of a xylophone.

"Didn't see you at Kelly's yesterday," Rusty said.

"No." Harlan squashed a match into the dock. "I was helping Libby pick out Grant's birthday gift."

"Turco ever get that necklace?"

Harlan nodded and took the joint back. "He's at the pier right now." He pinched the joint. "Talkin' to that guy Mars Bohr. You know him?"

"Yeah." Vay scratched sand from his hair. "I know him. Dude gets his shit hot."

"Yeah."

"All that pier shit is hot."

"Yep." Harlan took a drag of the marijuana and his eyes stung from smoke and he watched the smoke rise from the shuttle's boosters.

Rusty stared at Harlan's notebook. He asked him if he was putting down anything good.

"Yeah, I got some ideas." He mentioned the class and the teacher that had assigned him the book of Millay poems.

Rusty shook his head. He threw the thin knit hood over his face, cradling himself from the wind gusts. "I couldn't take that class, man." He kicked a pebble off the dock, into the foamy surge. "Shit's boring."

"It's not so bad."

"Yeah?"

Harlan nodded and a red glow fell over his face and he touched his cheeks. He said that he liked the class.

"That poetry shit?"

"I don't know."

"I can't read that shit, man."

"I guess I like the words."

"Not those kind."

Harlan mentioned a poem about the ocean and Rusty shrugged. "I guess, man. Stuff all sounds the same to me."

"I'm writing about my dreams."

"No shit."

"That's the poetry of existence. Dreams."

"Who told you that."

"The lady who teaches the class."

"The teacher then."

"I don't think she's a teacher. She just knows a lot about poetry."

It was cold and Rusty warmed his hands against the dock's metal railing. "So what's your dream about?"

Harlan thought about that and shrugged. "Not much of anything really. It's just a dream, a reoccurring dream. You ever have them?"

Rusty shook his head.

"There's this field," Harlan said. "Somewhere far off. Like a field in Scotland. But I can only see the high part of it."

"Like a glen."

"Yep. And on the high part of it, I can see that there's some light breaking cause it's that time between twilight and dark. And for awhile, I just freeze up because I'm afraid of what's over there but I don't want to run either. And on the high part of the field, I think I see someone there but there's not really anyone there but it's okay. I feel okay about it all cause the whole field is getting greener and full of light and sometimes in the dream I see that it is light that's breaking. And I'm going to head over there cause I hear the sound of surf on the other side."

"You know what's on the other side."

"Yeah, I do." He paused and watched the sky. He finally nodded because he was sure of it. "I do."

Rusty coughed, patting his jacket pockets. "I got another jay here somewhere." He went to search for the marijuana and the horizon suddenly went on fire as the shuttle gave lift-off. It appeared as a white chalk smear. The rockets echoed with a thunder that shook the dock and crows from the construction site became spooked by the sound and took to air.

Harlan studied its solitary ascent, growing smaller, meandering. He felt he could reach out and grab it. A beetle on patio screening.

The echo of rocket thunder spread across the sound, past the coastline, no longer a part of the landscape. It breathed across the stratosphere, becoming a small, white flame in a match. A thin line of contrail that rose into darker sky.

Rusty watched the horizon fill with afterburner. He put his hand over his eyes. He followed the Challenger's solitary flight. "Nice lift off."

Harlan stared at the white line of smoke. The smoldering ends curled and faded as the shuttle broke farther from the earth and it appeared like a small bottle rocket. He told Rusty that it was a beautiful lift-off and Rusty nodded.

Waves rippled against the dock and the crows were gone.

Sand from the construction yard blew across the dock and Harlan had to shield his eyes. The film of sand was followed by a breeze that cooled his sunburned skin and Harlan closed his eyes to it.